I0633318

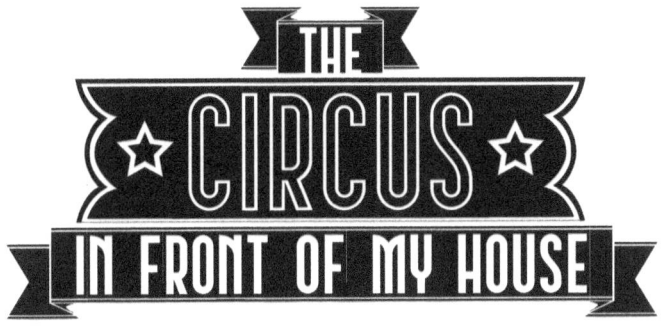

THE CIRCUS

IN FRONT OF MY HOUSE

a novel by **Adrian SANGEORZAN**

Translated from Romanian by Paul BOBOC

COPYRIGHT © 2022 by Adrian Sangeorzan
COVER DESIGN by Georgiana Oprescu
INTERIOR LAYOUT by Alexandru Oprescu

All rights reserved. Published by New Meridian, part of the non-profit organization New Meridian Arts, 2022.

No part of this publication may be reproduced, or stored in a retrieval system, or transmitted in any form or by any means, electronic, mechanical, photocopying, or otherwise, without written permission of the publisher, except in the case of brief quotations in reviews. For information regarding permission, write to newmeridianarts1@gmail.com

LIBRARY OF CONGRESS CATALOGING-IN-PUBLICATION DATA

The Circus in Front of My House
Authored by Adrian Sangeorzan
ISBN: 9781737249191
LCCN: 2022935996

Contents

Uncle Vili

I always liked clowns. Always confusing themselves and others, stepping awkwardly with their oversized shoes without doubting the nutty, upside-down world. The only world I knew. Until I turned 10, whenever I was asked what I wanted to become, I unhesitatingly answered: a clown. They seemed creatures blessed by fate to me. What more can you want than to entertain people? In return for your messy actions, your blunders and slightly sad face—things I could do without trying hard—you were rewarded with laughter and applause instead of being yelled at.

The first person I made laugh into uncontrollable stitches was Uncle Vili, the doctor in the village where my parents were teachers. Ever in a good mood, the edges of his lips naturally bent upward, despite the four years he spent at the Canal. Out of the twenty who'd been arrested in Stalin's day, only four ever came back. The other three had long forgotten how to laugh—you could tickle their soles, you could take them to any circus. When they got drunk they'd say that none would have stayed alive if Uncle Vili hadn't been among the doctors at the Canal. One of them was missing a leg. It had been crushed between two railway wagons. He'd passed out and been thrown alive into a public grave. Uncle Vili took him out of there that night and amputated his gangrened leg with whatever he had around, using a bottle of vodka as a disinfectant and anesthetic.

Himself having barely escaped death, Uncle Vili seemed like someone specially sent by fate, an ingenious wizard ever ready to raise the morale of people overwhelmed by fear, poverty and disease. No one knew or asked why he'd been arrested. This detail didn't concern anyone in a time when it was a public, almost patriotic duty to feel guilty. But for a while, we children were left out of this big cauldron where adults were boiled en masse in the seasoned soup of collective guilt.

When people talked about the Canal, they lowered their voices close to silence, using more of their arms and eyes instead. A canal that no one needed, abandoned before tying the Danube to the Black Sea—which, being a couple of feet higher than the river, would have flooded a large territory. The first Communist leader of Romania, Gheorghiu-Dej, supposedly complained to Stalin that he had too many subjects who opposed the regime. Stalin, disappointed that Romania didn't have a little Siberia, searched a map for an isolated zone and pointed his finger somewhere in the south.

"Make them dig a canal somewhere around here."

Uncle Vili was my uncle through a marriage with a cousin of my mother's, Aunt Uța, a beautiful and elegant woman with an interesting smile and a bearing that came from places that I could only imagine existed. Uncle Vili had become a well-known doctor in the area, a sort of legend. Sick people came to him from far away. He diagnosed me with low calcium and roundworms just by looking at my eyes and tongue. My stomach always hurt, and when I started growing, my knees would get weak, especially when I went up the hill to a school that didn't exactly draw me to it. He gave me injections that make me to have fever and I only went through this out of love for him. He was the first to realize that I was naturally a person that didn't have a good relationship with calcium, that brittle and whitish element that lodges in bones, but which shies from flowing through blood, muscles and nerves.

"When you're growing," he told me, "you need a lot of calcium."

Then he came to school with the vaccines, and I rolled my sleeve and was the first to leave my desk, like a true masochist.

He had become close to with my father, who cared for him as if he were for a brother.

They would go fishing together, walking around through the woods, where they'd pick mushrooms and talk about stuff I couldn't understand.

Sometimes they'd take me with them and they'd teach me how to tell a chub apart from a barbel, good mushrooms from poisonous ones, how to make fire without matches, how to build a cabin where no one can find you. I also found out—hearing things out—that we were going through hard times, that "this new eastern empire is worse than the old Austro-Hungarian one, people are getting to know how to betray one another and how to hate" and that "only the Americans can save us now."

Nothing went against what I learned in school, where my father was a professor and my mother a teacher, and where the teachers were never double-faced, never lied. I found out much later that my father too had been imprisoned, because he'd been a student of theology and that he refused to convert to Orthodoxy—even though he'd been a theology student. It was important which pew God's people prayed in. Sometimes they were serious to the point of scaring me, sometimes childish, as if all of life were a bad bet. On one of those journeys, I got to the top of a hill, and Uncle Vili told my father.

"That's where they shot my brother."

He said nothing, perhaps because I was instantly curious to find out who shot his brother and why, facts that he had no intention to share. He held no tragedy in himself, no hatred, no desire for revenge—just submission, mixed with helplessness. When Uncle Vili spoke about something serious, the edges of his lips would go down and he would raise his left eyebrow slightly, so slowly that it seemed a lazy curtain that would have revealed horrifying scenes to us had it gone higher.

Later, I found out that it took years for the Russians and new Communist militias to rid those mountains of the "enemies of the people" and of "peasants' black clothes." I had learned from my grandfather and great-grandfather that lawless people had hidden in those mountains since ancient times—they were named "haidouks." They recalled a certain Bosota, who attacked trains in the days of the Austro-Hungarians and robbed castles and manors with his gang. A bandit who had become popular and whose leg had been cut off to quiet him down. A haidouk with one leg was no longer dangerous. He was freed before he could be transformed into a martyr who might have been much more dangerous dead than alive. My great-grandfather had known him and drank with him at an inn in the mountains where the former haidouk, old and lame, would relate his life story to those who paid for his drinks.

Before the killing of his brother, who had himself become a well-known "bandit" and about whom Uncle Vili had no longer known anything for years, all of his relatives had been arrested and sent to the Canal to contribute to the unification of the Black Sea and Danube. But he had escaped from there. Those were

times in which martyrs or true heroes could no longer
be created, in which it was no longer enough to shorten
"enemies'" legs.

My parents, like the other intellectuals in the village, found out later that life could be beautiful too,
right then, in the '60s, when communism seemed a
continuous tide that allowed you to float if you didn't
go against it. They threw parties often, played cards,
laughed at nothing till late at night and seemed happy
that way. Something that was impossible for me to
understand. My sister and I were allowed to play under
the table, where we stared curiously at them, following
them as from a basement, where the adults' feet and
part of their helplessness could be seen. During one
party, they went outside to smoke. That night they had
praised the wine so much that they kindled our curiosity, and by the time they came back my sister and I had
emptied all the glasses on the table. The wine grandpa
made was so good and sweet that it put both of us into
a kind of alcoholic coma, which even Uncle Vili had
trouble getting us out of.

I had begun to feel that something wasn't all right
around me, something on a grand scale. A strange
double game was being played, a sort of continuous
scheme or mass hypnosis in which what was being
taken out of the hat didn't look like what we were seeing
in reality or had expected to see. What the adults said
out loud was never said when they were whispering. At
night, my folks spoke differently, listening to make sure

that my sister and I were asleep first. It seemed to me that they were afraid of us too, as if we were tiny spies who could put them in danger. I'd pretend to sleep so I could hear what they were saying. Maybe this is where my chronic and fickle insomnias come from.

All four of us slept in a large enclosure in the school building, with my grandma from my dad's side who joined us in the winter. My father also brought his motorcycle in the kitchen not to be stollen or frozen.

One night, I heard my mom saying that one of our relatives would slaughter an "undeclared" calf the next day. You weren't allowed to slaughter animals, even if they were yours, even if no meat could be found. "You can wind up at the Canal." The next day, after lots of whispered talk, they sent me with my schoolbag to bring meat in it. I made it beyond the valley carefully, so as not to make anyone suspicious. This time my knees didn't go soft. In this way, I was admitted into the secret circle of my family, which planned our survival. I'd proven to them that I could keep my mouth shut, silence in those days being the basic condition for inspiring trust and being taken in by smart folks.

Alongside the circus, our world was a continual amateur theater. Confusing, too abstract for children. Everything seemed a masquerade with foggy borders, imprecisely traced between ridiculousness, fun and the great danger that always grazed us.

Dad played Lenin once in a play. Short, bald, with his lively, genial stare, he seemed perfect for the role.

It was hardest with the goatee and mustache that dad didn't have and didn't want to grow. "I'll look so much like him that I'll be scared to look in the mirror." He took the role as a joke or farce, like the fake goatee and mustache, which Uncle Vili had made from the hair of an illegally slaughtered billy-goat. During his play-acting, these would come off, and dad would mess up his lines trying to put them back. Toward the end, he simply held them in his hand, lisping quietly and seriously so as not to burst out laughing. Now, Lenin no longer seemed convinced of what he was saying; what's more, with his hand on his mouth, he seemed like a person that would have wanted to hide his enormities. Uncle Vili laughed openly in a roar. I restrained myself, since Lenin was my father, after all, and the audience lay suspended between joy and fear, finally clapping shily. Mom, who had directed the show, told Uncle Vili over my head:

"Stop laughing or they'll arrest us all."

For me, Lenin always remained a big clown, a tragi-comic figure of the world. When I saw him in 1988 in his mausoleum in Moscow, I felt like laughing. I stayed in a ridiculously long line that no one forced me to stay in, though I was still far from being a free man. His tiny beard seemed like an impaled billy-goat's, and he seemed like one of the seven dwarves, lost in a horrific fairy-tale where he'd been elected emperor by mistake. Communism had become a dusty decorum, forgotten on a stage on which actors had begun to speak without holding their hands over their mouths. I still ask those who go there whether they keep him in the mausoleum like that, rigid, his hands on his chest, as if he were the caricature of a pharaoh who wants to frighten people—even the dead.

The son of the most celebrated teacher, I was later selected for the school's shows. My first role was Harap Alb, a neutral, mythological character who fought with the forces of evil while in love with Ileana Cosânzeana, a princess. Her role was played by a girl from the Hungarian section—Ildiko, the miller's daughter whom I loved in secret. I had an imperial paper crownet on my head; on my waist a wooden sword that I'd made myself. I wore a princely costume made of crepe paper, covering my short pants and thin legs, which Uncle Vili's calcium hadn't taken over yet. Before the show I went out to the schoolyard to play, overwhelmed by the role and all the props on me. A sudden summer storm came and when I got on stage, our national colors, drenched in wet paper, started to flow down my face and legs. The biggest problem involved the miller's daughter, who gave me her replies well before I finished my own. When she forgot them in Romania, she'd say them in Hungarian. My lines were always being cut off, and at one point I told her, irritated:

"Come on, you say it all." Then she grew completely quiet. I laughed stupidly and spoke the famous reply, like a miniature Hamlet:

"You're laughing now, Harap Alb, but it's not your laughter," an expression that had long since become a commonplace saying among Romanians.

Uncle Vili laughed himself to stitches in the back of the hall—a healthy though delicate laughter, so as not to hurt me in any way. I saw his joyful, flushed face, and I was as happy as a strange clown that I'd been able to make him joyful. At the end, I recited a stupid poem about our beloved party that guarded our child-hoods. It had to end patriotically and in an apotheosis. I messed up some things in each verse, worsening the situation. I finished the poem hurriedly, quietly, inton-ing it doubtfully, as if there were a big question mark in front of every affirmation. When I finished, I wanted to run offstage, but my teacher stopped me:

"You forgot to bow."

I went back and bowed deeply, but with my butt toward the public. Then the tense audience exploded in applause. I bowed again, deeper, and I glanced at them all through my legs. Upside-down as they were, they seemed silly to me, and I started to laugh too.

"You need to become a clown," Uncle Vili told me. He hugged me, gave me 10 lei and promised me that he'd take me to Bistriţa someday to the circus.

They took me to Bistriţa, a city I'd long dreamed of reaching, right after I'd been welcomed into the ranks of the Motherland's pioneers. I took this seriously—fixing the red tie and the pioneers' badge—as a true symbol of my ideological enrolment into a serious, solid organization. They let me walk by myself on Corso, with my fire-like red tie, and for some reason I felt like going inside a church. Maybe I wanted to express my gratitude, an "Angel, my little angel," the only prayer I knew by heart. A priest with a long beard, who stood by the entrance like a pillar of faith, stopped me:

"Boy, it's not good for you to come into the Lord's house with that red thing around your neck." He hampered me totally, and I ran left and right, bewildered. It was my first ideological conflict, and I settled it pretty quickly. Later, I came across a group of older boys, with bags on their backs, and I saluted them seriously with my hand against my forehead:

"A joyful pioneer's salute!"

"Up your mother's!" they answered, and with this it was over with the red tie and the pioneers.

Les Miserables and Vava

Behind the school I attended, lived in and played in was the train station. With the replacing of the old locomotives and trains, they had to change the railroad, the rails, beams, rocks between them and everything having to do with the iron road. They lived in wagons and barracks and seemed more like people condemned to forced labor than soldiers that one might have presumed were trained to defend their fatherland. Me and my neighbors, Martin Wolf and Yohli, were there every evening and quickly made friends with some of them. But we were told to be careful, because they were a disciplinary battalion of soldiers "with problems."

Vava and Jean were unbreakable, and that summer I grew as close to them as to two older brothers. Especially Vava, a joyful, friendly boy from a southern city. He spoke Romanian differently from us, with a different accent and much more quickly. I understood everything he said, but he had problems with the language I spoke. I had to explain to him that a "palant" is a fence, "glaja" glass and other words that he noted amusedly in a notebook. He had a long face, the traces of childhood still well-preserved in eyes that always laughed somewhat naively. Only his muscular and tall body and his Adam's apple, which seemed to come out of his long neck, made him look manly.

It was hard for me to keep up with them at first. They often used rare and big words, unusual for me, such as: incredible, plausibly, malady, onanism and abstinence. When I asked them what onanism is, Vava told me sadly that it's what they do there at night because of abstinence. What's abstinence? It's a lack. Lack of what? Well, of everything—food, drink, books and women. The "fundamental" needs in a real man's life. I skipped the women, whom I had no idea how to obtain, and I began to bring them food and books from home at night, since I had enough. Sometimes I'd slip them a bottle of beer or vodka.

My folks allowed me to go to the improvised military unit, because those there were all "political," half soldiers, half prisoners, almost all the sons of the former bourgeoisie and rich, traditional enemies of the people, like Uncle Vili. They wore used, discolored uniforms, and I never saw them getting trained or carrying guns. The armed ones were a couple real soldiers in new uniforms, very green, who guarded them somewhat formally and weren't too friendly.

The first book I brought them was Victor Hugo's *Les Miserables*, and Jean asked me whether I had the French edition at home. We all burst out laughing. Jean was the most serious and most educated among them, seldom smiled, looked elegant even in that shabby uniform and shaved twice a day for no reason. It was over with French and French things. At school they were trying to teach us Russian, a coarse language whose words we avoided as instinctively as a saw's teeth. As if that language had brought all our troubles upon us.

I hadn't read any book yet, as it was work that I disliked deeply. My folks tried by force to make me read, locking me periodically in my room with a chair and storybook. A simple one with pictures, whose subject-matter I would then have to relate. Eventually I'd look at the pictures to make something up, then play with jam jars with which I'd make a pyramid, or eat pickles until they'd let me out. Out of fear that I'd ruin their winter reserves, they stopped pressuring me with lectures, predicting instead that I'd become "uncultured," a word that left me cold even after Uncle Vili kindly explained it to me.

The four volumes of *Les Miserables* went from hand to hand until half the battalion had read it. They gave them back torn, their covers wrapped in newspapers sheets, the official and stupid publication of our popular army which fixed the rails. I always heard them discussing the book; I understood nothing and promised myself angrily that they'd never see any more books from me. They were calling Jean Jean-Valjean now, and when I asked Vava why they gave him that nickname he told me:

"You read the book, too. I'm sure you'll understand. If you don't get something, ask me."

The second morning, when they were working with their pickaxes and I had no one to play with, I picked up the first volume and opened it fearfully. And I was right. Books, as I'd find out later, have their own traps. It was hardest with the first page, then I read all four volumes. Greedily, slowly, re-reading favorite pages, day by day, till the evening, when they returned from the barracks and I from an imaginary world where I treaded passioned in the footsteps of the real Jean-Valjean. It was my first book. Outside of Bistrița I had never been anywhere, and suddenly I'd made a "fabulous" discovery of the mental journey, which no one can take away from you.

Mom observed the change, and when she was making pancakes she'd send some to the boys at the railroad, and dad sent them cigarettes. One Sunday we invited them over to eat, and even though they weren't allowed to leave the barracks, they slipped through the orchard, and my folks treated them like true guests. They invited me later to a film that played in a wagon, a film about Russian partisans. In the wagon they smoked heavily, and on the screen the partisans smoked. It was so smoky there you could cut the air with a knife, so they barely noticed when the first woman appeared on the screen, a partisan in a thick padded coat with an automatic on her shoulder.

"Attention, attention, the scene is coming now!" cried someone who'd seen the movie before. The woman took off her bonnet from her head, letting her long blonde hair fall back. Then she took out her automatic and coat, revealing a well-shaped form, through which the heavy chest of a Soviet woman showed. The hall began to grow agitated; comments flew in undertones by my ears, and the boys could hardly control themselves when she started to unbutton her coat slowly, staring into the emptiness, her mind on her duties. She had just gotten to her second button when the wretched Ivan came in, her fighting comrade, who made her button herself up. Before we all fizzled, they jumped into one-another's arms and kissed for a long time.

Unfortunately, the scene was filmed from behind Ivan, so at the forefront you mostly saw the Kalashnikov automatic; their lips couldn't be seen at all, and I would have liked to see what they were doing with them. "Come on, fuck her..." cried someone in the back, and Vava got up on his feet and yelled at him: "You idiot, can't you see there's a child here?" I felt doubly humiliated, though I'd assisted with the first love scene, lightly pornographic according to Soviet standards.

Vava confessed to me that he had a lover who waited for him there, in the South. It was a complicated relationship, with parents who hated each other; her father, after becoming a big boss, forbade her to so much as think about him. He showed me her picture, an absolutely beautiful girl, and he asked me to help him get in contact with her. He wrote her long letters that I put in the mail, and she answered via our address, using my name. In this way they avoided the censorship, or at least so they thought.

The mailman asked me one day, looking at me suspiciously, how it was that at my age I had a lover who wrote me from so far away. I didn't give him any reckoning. I took the letter, climbed a chair and put it next to the bulb that hanged from the ceiling, the first form of electricity that I'd ever come into contact with. "My dear Adrian," I succeeded in reading between the superimposed words onto the pages. Although I knew it wasn't addressed to me, I must confess that I felt flattered, like a fool. There followed, with a few relational expressions between them, different variations on the words "love", "affection", "waiting", etc. which repeated ad infinitum, making me believe that love might be a heavy, incurable disease, especially since the letter closed with "I will wait for you as long as I must, if I must, until death." After this, I didn't even bother to see what else she wrote. I would take the letters to Vava, who would rip them from my hand and read them breathlessly. After which he would re-read them with tears in his eyes, while mine rolled bored, waiting for him to come back from his trance.

Sometimes I played the clown, miming tender love scenes and imaginary kisses. He didn't find it particularly funny, but I did my best to dissipate his melancholy, which seemed to affect his sense of humor. We played soccer on the maidan, and he lay under a tree and wrote poems with and without rhymes. Sometimes he'd read them to me and ask me what I thought about them. I didn't know what to say. He would cry for me and ask me to give him a rhyme, and I was very good at this.

Even now, I remember a fragment of poetry that began with: "The rails of the railway have begun to bring forth buds." Worrisome, isn't it? I realized then, though nothing had happened to me yet, that love is a dangerous game that turns people upside-down and transforms them completely until it makes them unrecognizable. If he'd come to see the rails of the railroad budding, it's no wonder that one day one of them fell over his shoulder and dislocated it badly while he was unloading them from a wagon. In the evening they took him out on a stretcher, sighing in pain, his swollen arm bound to his body. They had a medical assistant there who had no idea what to do with him, and that's when I came forward and told the captain that I have an uncle who's a doctor in the village.

They lifted him onto the only car they had, a military jeep. Together with me and a real armed soldier, we all went to the medical dispensary. Uncle Vili had finished his shift and was tying some vines that had climbed up to the roof with dad. When they saw the military jeep and the armed soldier, they both froze. They reflexively remembered their own arrests, the days when they'd been manacled and given for lost. They came to their senses only when they saw me getting off with Vava, who was in visible pain. Uncle Vili took Vava inside and took everyone out, with the exception of myself, who had procured his patient. He examined Vava, smiling in a friendly way, and he told him that he had a serious dislocation in his shoulder that he could fix on the spot.

"But I don't have any anesthetics and it'll hurt you! Do you think you can endure it?" Vava looked at me scared, as if I might have had a solution. Uncle Vili brought a bottle of brandy from the house and filled a large glass. "This will help you!" Vava drank it with difficulty, hiccupping, and when he finished the glass, he looked cross-eyed, smiled crookedly and seemed ready for any intervention. Uncle Vili stretched him out on a table, took his sick hand smiling, as if he were congratulating him warmly for some accomplishment, propped one of his feet on his right armpit, and before we could guess what he wanted to do, he pulled strongly on the sprained arm, which started to crackle and creak like an unoiled hinge. A click was heard, as if the bone had gone back into articulation, like a closing door. Vava stopped groaning. His pain disappeared.

"That's it, boy. Want some more brandy?"

Vava seemed half-unconscious and spoke with difficulty.

"And what do you say your name is?"

Vava spelled out his last name, and Uncle Vili began asking him about his family.

"Mother is a literature teacher in Constanța. Father was a military man by profession and died at the Canal."

After a long pause during which he bandaged his arm and set it back on his body, Uncle Vili said in a low, calm tone:

"I knew your father well. I was close to him when he died. He always spoke about you."

No one said anything else, and the others came to take Vava, who had suddenly returned from drunkenness and pain. Outside he staggered, vomited several times and looked even more upside down than his stomach. I remained alone with Uncle Vili, who spoke to me for the first time like an adult:

"Vava's father was one of the brightest Romanian officers. He was a close friend of mine at the Canal. I'd like to see your friend again."

I ran to the car and told them that the doctor would have to change the bandage every two days. They saw each other many times after that and I'd stay outside, in the waiting room, leaving them alone. Vava would come out with tears in his eyes, but he seemed happy.

"He tells me things about my father that I didn't know."

Vava's accident had its good side too. I could spend entire days with him. Being incapable of work, he'd sit with me on the edge of the railroad on a mound from where you could see the whole village. He couldn't write anymore, so he started dictating his love letters and poems to me. As Vava's scribe, I learned my first rules in the composition of epistles. The date, then always "My love," an introduction, the content, and the ending which was always dramatic. And I especially learned lots of new words, which he explained with much joy and in detail. One day, I told my mother that the onion she had just cut reeked "pestilentially."

I'd lie down under an apple tree with my notebook and pencil, and he'd stroll in front of me with his arm in his scarf and dictate. He passed swiftly and unexpectedly from prose to poetry and vice versa, like the trains that interrupted us once in a while, which passed so close to us that we didn't budge an inch, like mimes. I proposed to him to climb the hill, or to walk in the woods around. He would remind me that his freedom was very limited. After a month he got better and went back to his pickaxe work. I'd gotten used in the meantime to his epistolary style, so that I could write his lover by myself.

One of the letters I brought him one day turned him upside down so badly that he became unrecognizable. He almost didn't speak at all, and his voice drowned whenever he tried to utter a word. He didn't laugh anymore, and neither did he feel the need to write. Not even Jean-Valjean knew what had happened to him. "Women," he said, "eternally to blame."

One morning, mom came home upset, having failed to find my father's shirt and pants on a rope she stretched to dry the clothes. I noticed that next to us, at the barracks, the soldiers hadn't left their work and there was great excitement. Rarely did you hear the trumpet announce a gathering. Now it was sounding desperately, and they were all lined up in straight rows. I approached Jean, who was at the edge of the column, and he whispered to me horrified, between his teeth:

"Vava has disappeared!"

Not knowing what to do, I ran down the railroad and went to the tree under which Vava dictated the letters. A piece of paper was stuck to a bayonet; Vava had written on it: "Forgive me for leaving so abruptly. May your family forgive me for the clothes I took. I'll write you one day." There was much desperation in those words. A train passed by; the mechanic saw that I was too close to the tracks and pulled the horn, filling the valley with a long cry like the groan of a huge animal. There the trains climbed up slopes, locomotives with steam panting heavily, obese and old, slowing down. Some of the travelers stuck their heads out of the windows and would snatch apples from the branches that almost touched the train. I was sure that Vava had jumped on one of the freight trains that always passed by.

It was harder for me to go into the barracks, and Jean asked me to tell him if I ever got news from Vava. He didn't write me, and no letters came his way.

Two weeks later they returned him in handcuffs, badly beaten up. First a special car that stopped at the barracks appeared, a Russian Volga I think, something unheard of in the village, then the unit's jeep from which they took him, and they threw him directly into the wagon where I knew the detention barracks were located. They didn't let me go in, but after the darkness settled, I went around the barracks, went through an apple orchard, and hidden in the tall grass, I approached the detention-wagon. The guard patrolled along the rail, and I succeeded in slipping through that cage that's at the end of every wagon. I was able to see Vava through a small opening. He lay on a wooden bed and scratched the wall of his cell with his handcuffs. In fact, he was writing, scribbling with metal on metal words that would be hard to erase. I cried to him in a low voice and he turned his head as if he'd had a hallucination. He got close to the place where I was and I saw his bruised face, his swollen eye and cracked lips.

"It's me, don't be afraid!" There was no way he could see me, even though he had gotten so close to the wall that I could feel his breathing. It was like I was at a confession.

"What did they do to you?"

"They caught me, boy. I was almost away, at the Danube, ready to pass over to the Serbs in Yugoslavia. Mom died, and my girlfriend is marrying another man. Only the words didn't betray me."

The door of the cabin opened suddenly, and I saw the barrel of a gun pointing at me.

"Stay or I'll shoot!" shouted the idiot of a soldier.

After he recognized me, he pulled me down, slapped me, kicked me and told me that if he found me again there he'd shoot me.

I ran home with my heart beating powerfully and hid in the cellar. I wept and ate lots of apples without being hungry or wanting them. I ate them with hatred and struck the stubs against the walls. It was the first time that I felt the bitter taste of helplessness, though those apples were sweet and guiltless. Then I went outside, filled my pickets with rocks and approached the barracks. It was an early fall evening, with a full moon. Dad and mom had come out worried and looked at me soberly without saying anything, without trying to stop me. They wanted to see what a furious kid would do, the only person left who could have thrown stones into a system they couldn't oppose. I threw a single stone as hard as I could, and I heard it fall somewhere close to Vava's barracks. I emptied my pockets, convinced of the uselessness of my protest. I went back home, and my folks were very good with me that evening.

Vava disappeared suddenly from my life. He was sent to a court martial, condemned, and had to serve hard years in prison. I never heard of him again. I read *Papillon* about three times and I always saw Vava as the detainee who would surely escape one day and write me from an exotic country. I continued to imagine communism like that island in French Guyana. Barren, isolated, cliffy, where wrongfully condemned people served life sentences. Without the possibility of escape, free only to gaze hopelessly at the sky and the endless ocean.

The Americans
and Mineral Waters

After dad and Uncle Vili bought two motorcycles, they became almost inseparable. "Now we can go wherever we want, whenever want" they would say, and they'd leave to Borsec, a mountain resort "very far away," meaning about a hundred kilometers away. There, they both treated their gastric ulcers. Uncle Vili's from the Canal, my father's from a communist prison. They had almost a cult-like obsession with the mineral waters there, and their ulcers became magical diseases over time, about which they spoke respectfully and with humor. Whenever I'd complain about a stomachache later on, dad would tell me worriedly: "Be careful not to develop an ulcer. That's all we need." He had a certain tone of voice whenever he said this. I had to understand that generally things had to be taken seriously. Everything had to be done carefully, with a neat carelessness, studied, a trade that is not so easy to learn. Their ulcers were obviously the result of a much too large sediment of worries and misfortunes, deposited exactly where it shouldn't have been. Plus the food at random hours, on the run, cold, moldy and especially poorly chewed. He would add all of this, staring at me as I ate fast, ready to go play.

When they went with their motorcycles to the mineral water treatment, they'd take me and my sister to our grandparents on my mother's side, at Bârla, a village several kilometers away. There, it was more country-like like in the old times. Only the peasants' strange sandals, called "*opinci*," now made from the rubber of former car and tractor wheels, made you think that things were happening more recently. The Communists hadn't been able to seize all their goods to collectivize them completely yet, even though collectivization had been reported as over throughout the whole country. They still let them work the land, but they taxed the harvest with more than they could keep up with. This to convince them "nicely."

My grandparents would say that it was much worse than in the days of the Hungarian nobles and, with my four grandparents, who were still alive, they spoke more freely in our presence. They had nothing to be afraid of anymore. They would even take us to church on Sunday to convince us that God wasn't dead yet and that the help could only come from that direction.

Grandma kept all the fasts and prayed for hours on end in front of a glass icon, through which his eye surely saw us, more and more disgusted by the lawlessness and wrongs that were happening to us. The expressions she used most often were "Don't let them, Lord" and "Help us, help us." I was sure that her prayers protected us too, so that we didn't have to worry too much. I was a little scared to sit in front of that icon, which (among other things) had a big eye painted on it, which seemed to stare at me pretty indifferently. Later, an icon collector wanted to buy it, but grandma had nothing to do with money anymore, either.

A kid called for me one day, very dispraisingly: "Hey, you rich peasant's chick!" I asked my grandpa what a rich peasant was. "Someone like me," he answered. I went out into the street and for the first time I picked a fight, so that our neighbors, also poor rich peasants, had to separate us. That fall they took their lands, animals and tools. They only left them their house, a small yard around it, a cow, the dog, cat and bees.

"It's hard to nationalize bees," grandpa used to say. Maybe they'd have done it, those bastards, had they known that bees have a queen. The peasants hadn't yet forgotten their former king, long since exiled, and not Queen Maria either. Sometime, around the month of May, grandpa was pouring wine into his glass and just like that, out of nowhere, raised the glass to the poor king who was God knows where on his birthday.

Grandpa also had a piece of vineyard, up on a slop-ing hill, which they'd forgotten to confiscate. This gave him a bit of faith in the future. When they took their land, he got drunk for the first time, and when he got up from his drunkenness, he said that we have to look at the bright side:

"We'll work much less, we'll learn to steal what was once ours and we'll sit on the porch, to see who passes by."

To console him, dad and Uncle Vili bought him a radio where he listened to foreign channels from Ger-many and America. When grandma prayed, he'd cry out to her:

"Don't forget to pray to Him for the Americans to come!"

"Will the Americans really come?" I would ask him.

"I don't think anyone's coming."

Another person who waited for the Americans was my great grandfather from my grandmother's side, Old Man Mora. Much of the land that they'd had taken away from them had been bought from dollars brought by them from America in the four or five "expeditions" there, during and after the first world war. He believed in the Americans, though he'd never gotten a chance to understand them or to understand their gibberish. He'd worked in a factory in Cleveland, whose name he pronounced very phonetically. Whenever he fathered some money and missed his home, he'd cross the ocean to buy a piece of land and leave grandma pregnant.

He'd go back before she was due to give birth. One of many Transylvanian peasants, weird commuters between continents at the beginning of the century. They were called "the Americans."

Sunday, they'd sit together at church and at the dance, leaning on canes with silver knobs brought from Cleveland. Old Man Mora died in a winter, two days after grandma, and they buried them at the same time. He was our last "American." The village madman, a poor mentally retarded fellow, uninhibited and fearless, would say at the inn that "the Americans have left, now there's no one left to come."

After collectivization, grandpa, overwhelmed by so much new free time, started to read and even to write poetry. Simple, in popular verses. And then he and his father, my great-grandfather, filled my head with happenings that they thought they'd forgotten. Stories that went way back, stories with long legs that had stepped, with their soles, in the Middle Ages, much too prolonged in that part of the world. I would have liked to provoke them more, especially grandpa, who felt his end drawing near. I called him Old Dad. He died in a summer when I was vacationing with them. He was around 90; no one kept track of his years anymore and, like everyone who dies a natural death, he was sure he'd feel it when the angels would flap on his shoulders. He called on us twice to say goodbye. Grandma had to arrange his pillow under his bed each time, and an icon on his chest, and we each lit a candle and waited patiently for death to come and take him. He died for good on the third try and grandma put a mirror over his face again, to see whether it would get foggy.

"This time he's gone," she said.

Not understanding what she was doing with the mirror, I stooped and stared into its luster, waiting to see death take him or at least that eye that sees and knows everything. Back then I was afraid of death. The old folks had convinced me that it's a temporary state, that we'd all resurrect one day and find each other just as we'd been. I'd become a believer, without the questions and doubts that started to trouble me later on.

The Neighbors, Kennedy and the End of the World

Uncle Vili's death was a shock for us all. He had gotten leukemia, which finished him off in a month. This event made me understand that death can come just like that, out of the blue, like summer rain, whenever things are going best for you. Dad sat by him until he faded away. He didn't have an existential crisis, he joked calmly and smiled to everyone until he closed his eyes like one who'd seen death many times and understood that he'd had only a temporary reprieve. My father's ulcer was gone by then, but he developed a kind of depression, which was much worse. He smoked much, he was sad and didn't hear us when we spoke, as if he'd gone deaf. He left with mom to Borsec, convinced still of the universal forces of those mineral waters and the strong mountain air.

When they got back, they informed us that we'd move as soon as possible to Bistriţa, the closest city to us, where we had lots of relatives. I was glad that we were going to the city. I'd gotten tired of Şieu, a village where people either died or went to surreal countries like Palestine, Germany or America, places whose existence I doubted for a long time, as if they were territories from the netherworld.

No one asked the Germans or Jews whether they'd leave. It went without saying. The suspects for us were those who didn't leave. After long expectations and prevarication, they were allowed to emigrate or, better yet, to disappear quietly, without too much of a fuss about shaking hands, so as not to plant wild and melancholy desires in the others' souls. Only Romanians and Hungarians couldn't go anywhere. No one traveled in those days, no one moved. Back then, when people left, they left *definitively*, like Uncle Vili or the Roşu family.

The Roşu brothers were my best friends in Şieu. I was about ten when they left to Palestine. I only heard about Israel later on. Yohli, the oldest, and the one with whom I got along the best, had told me that there, in Palestine, you'd get four oranges for a potato. An impressive exchange rate. I'd eaten oranges only twice in my life and they were unbelievable. I was forced to eat potatoes every day.

The Roşu brothers were four boys who came one after the other. I played all day long with them. That was the first time that a separation hurt me and I couldn't understand why they had to leave. Anyway, the thing with the four oranges for a potato was the only motivation that stood strong for me. A little before them, the Lehman family left, which had a boy, Andrew. For them, Palestine was only a stop. They wrote my parents from America, but they didn't mention anything about the exchange rate of potatoes and oranges there.

The Wolf family, which lived near the railroad, went to Germany, a place that was easier to find for me, and where potatoes could be exchanged for potatoes.

Words stuck easily to my ears. I'd started understanding German, Hungarian, even Yiddish. No one could swear at me in any of the languages that were being spoken over my head.

We lived near the railroad, right in the school where my parents were teachers. The school was in the former estate of a Hungarian nobleman. It was totally unfunctional, with a huge unused cellar where we played in secret. But we played best in the synagogue that had been abandoned some good years past. All its windows were broken, its doors stolen, and it rained through the roof. The Roşu family was the last family of Jews that remained in the village and lived right in the yard of the synagogue, which they'd cared for before. Now they had nothing left to take care of except the sweet potatoes in the back of the yard.

The evangelical German church was between the estate—that is, the school—and the synagogue that was right by the road. The church bothered us most

in the winter when we took our sleds down and had
to go around it.

The house where the Roşu family lived had only
two tiny rooms, where only they could possibly have
known how they lived. They were very poor and for
two years had waited to leave, day after day. I liked to
eat there in the evening, bread grilled on the furnace
and rubbed with garlic and butter. Mrs. Roşu said that
the garlic was healthy and protected us from roundworms. On Christmas, when we cut the pig, mother
sent them sausages and puddings, and on Easter, cakes
and red eggs. On Passover they would send us *matzo*.

There were things that only we boys did, like bathing in the river in summertime, butt naked. We'd go
with the Roşu brothers to the brook and get naked
in the bushes. I was amazed the first time I saw their
circumcised penises. They looked nothing like mine,
which was flabby and hairless, with a hoodie on its
head. And I caught them peeking over at me, too. That's
when I noticed that there are differences between us
also. Otherwise, we all wiped our noses with the back
of our hands and wore the same kind of boots, always
re-soled. No one said anything then, but when I got
home, I asked my folks:

"Why do the Roşu brothers have different cocks?"

My folks stared at me in silence, then glanced at
one another. I hadn't given them time to devise a more
elaborate answer. They knew that once they said something, for me it would be like the end of a string that

I'd start pulling. As teachers they couldn't allow themselves half-baked answers, especially not to their kid.

"It's something related to their religion," dad told me vaguely. "It's called circumcision."

"Meaning? What's a circumcision? Why does it happen? How does it happen? Why don't I have such a thing?"

Dad continued to grade the students' quizzes, suddenly very busy. Mom hurried strategically to the kitchen, where she suddenly had something cooking.

"You'd do better to ask them," dad said. "You're friends, after all."

Which is what I did. They also wanted to ask me what was up with my cock. But the problem remained unsolved, due to a lack of responsibility on the part of the four parents and of our somewhat limited interest. Back then we were very into archery and dueling with wooden swords. It was during the '60s at the village's community center and they were showing the first swashbuckler French-Italian films. We practiced best around the German church, which high up, on its spire, had a metal globe instead of a cross.

The man we also went to war with was Herr Martin, the old man who cared for the church and tolled the bells every day. We thought he hated us, because he always chased us away, threatening us with his cane. We'd heard that during the war he'd been a Nazi, and we saw him like in those Russian movies with guerilla fighters, wearing a metallic helmet and an automatic hanging on his neck. In fact, he had a wooden leg with which he returned from Russia, where he'd been a prisoner for ten years. When he came thumping with his leg, we all ran for our lives.

The conflict began when one of my arrows took a wrong turn. I'd aimed at a thick poplar that, gracefully, hid itself in time, and my arrow was found Sunday, in the German church, stuck in a pew. No one summoned the militia or other special forces. The German priest understood that it was in fact only an arrow that someone had lost control of. Dad confiscated my arrow, and my only weapon left was the wooden sword. So as not to lose our eyes, we pilfered our parents' sunglasses. I would give Yohli a pair and we'd duel fiercely. The other Roşu brothers, my sister and the Wolf brothers umpired. We'd thrust with our left hands just like in the movies, careful not to hurt ourselves. Once, we awoke with Mr. Martin about a meter away from us, with his cane raised. This time he was smiling and held it like a sword. The other children ran like lightning. I was petrified, but we both stayed there, determined not to sell ourselves cheap. But Mr. Martin was cheerful and was laughing at us.

"Hey, kids, you don't knowing how to duel good. If you no more break the church windows, I teach at you."

We really weren't expecting this at all. In front of the church entrance there was a cast cement plate. He took a piece of broken tile and drew a line in the cement. He had me sit to the side of the line, and he sat on the other side.

"Now attack at me," he said.

He was using his cane like a sword and he moved with unexpected accuracy. He gave us explanations regarding the body's position, lunging, how to defend, how to attack, and so on. These were the rule even before the first world war when he (so he said) had fought in duels twice somewhere in the Austria-Hungary of those days.

"Did you kill them in the duels?" we asked, frightened.

"No," he answered. "Just small wounds on them, and a lot of shame."

We believed everything he said and starting that day, Mr. Martin assumed mythical proportions for us. We no longer cried after him "Mr. Martin walks with his trousers."

On a rainy day, when I was alone, and he was coming to toll the evening bells, I asked him to take me with him up to the belfry of the church. I knew the melody of the three bells by heart, but I'd never been there.

"Gut. Komm mit mir!" Good, come with me, he said, and I climbed the narrow steps behind him, in a spiral, which he thumped on with his wooden leg. I wanted to ask him whether the God of the Germans was the same as ours or the Hungarians' or the Jews', but I changed my mind. Adults can become weird when you ask them about sacred things, as if each prayed to something else, which is what I think they do after all, despite all churches having bells. It wasn't clear to me why the synagogue didn't have its own bells.

The bells' ropes were about three meters under them. Mr. Martin pulled them like a professional, not allowing me to touch anything yet. My ears rang and my chest vibrated like a drum. I understood why he couldn't hear too well. I put my hands on my ears and looked at the village through a narrow crack in the bell-tower's wall, with a feeling of exaltation.

"Don't tell anyone I take you up here. Gut?"

I kept my mouth shut till the evening, when I told Yohli everything. I went up to the spire several more times with Mr. Martin. I liked the vibration of the nearby big bell and the image of the village as seen from up high.

Yohli the curious and circumcised couldn't resist it any longer. He pleaded with me, timidly, to speak with Mr. Martin to take him to the bell-tolling too. At least once. He had no idea why their synagogue wasn't equipped with the same thing. He promised me his skates in return. He had only one skate, and a weird one at that, crooked at the tip, which he tied in the winter with ropes on a boot and with which he drove the sled from ahead. I think he suspected that he wouldn't catch the following winter there.

I had to use all my cleverness to convince Mr. Martin. He seemed disconcerted and amused at the same time.

"Aber, he's a Jew, no?" he said at one point.

"And?" I shrugged my shoulders.

"Gut. If this is what he wants, *warum nicht?* Why not? Aber really won't say anything about this to anyone. Do you swear on your sword?" he answered solemnly.

"I swear," I answered him, my hand on my heart. I went up with Yohli behind him, step by step, and I saw that my friend was pretty nervous. When the bells started to ring, he got pretty scared, and I told him to put his hands over his ears. We glanced at each other and at the village, which seemed like a tame animal asleep between the hills. After we got down from there, Yohli made me swear on the same wooden sword that I wouldn't mention anything about this to his folks. I respected my promises.

Mr. Martin did weird things. That winter, he was the one who killed Santa Claus out of carelessness. For me it was less painful than for my sister. After decorating the tree, mom, having no alternatives, called on Mr. Martin to pretend to be Santa. They put as much makeup on his as they could, but we recognized him immediately from his German accent and the thumping of his wooden leg. Two years after that, one night, I heard the owl singing from the church's bell tower. That's when I knew that Mr. Martin had died.

One day, Yohli looked for me at home and told me that they were ready to leave. He didn't seem too happy. His folks had finally been summoned by the authorities and their passports had been handed to them. Palestine was waiting for them in a week. That night I couldn't sleep. The following day I avoided them, and on the third I asked them if I could sleep that night at their place. They had all their boxes filled in the middle of the room. Only the furnace was in its usual place and the earthenware tied to the wall. They were all quiet, even scared. They made the same grilled bread with garlic and sweet baked potato on the furnace. The parents then went to the so-called bedroom with the youngest kids. The rest of us were to sleep on two empty mattresses thrown on the floor. It reeked strongly of garlic and naphthalene. We didn't speak much, and no one really felt like laughing. Yohli promised to write me. It got past midnight, and we couldn't fall asleep and we whispered to one another.

"I want to show you something," he said mysteriously at one point. Then he signaled me to be quiet and slowly opened an old closet that was almost crumbling. He took a brown leather bag out of it, all nibbled at the edges. He opened it slowly and showed me some weird, rusty instruments inside it. I didn't understand anything. Then he took one of them and laid it implicitly next to his cock. Then he made the sign of cutting around it. Aha, I finally understood almost everything, and I didn't ask for any more explanations. Two days later they left, and Yohli had a Bar Mitzva in Israel, in a kibbutz with orange trees.

Pretty much every Christmas, when we decorated the tree with apples, biscuits and colored candy, Yohli would send me a postcard with palm trees. They were doing well there, where it was hot, but I don't know if they'd ever gotten around to getting four oranges for a potato.

Several years later, my father received a letter from Mr. Roşu. In it there was a piece of newspaper in

Romanian, with Yohli's picture showing him almost grown into a man. He had been killed during the Six-Days War.

In those years I think that seed of uprooting cornered me, that desire to move from one place to another, feeling like an exile and prisoner where I wound up.

President Kennedy was assassinated in the same summer. I found out the horrible news coming down from my grandparents' at Bârla. I say horrible because that's how it was portrayed to me by Grigore, a kind of uncle who came back drunk with his carriage from Şieu. His rod in his hand, venting mindlessly on an innocent horse, only flesh and bones, he was fuming and cursing like a cabman. When he saw me, he stopped his vehicle which was ready to break apart and called to me from a cloud of smoke and brandy mist:

"If you see your dad tell him that's it's over with the Americans and with us all. It's the end of the world, boy."

He was very congested in the face and spoke with difficulty, drunk as he was, but he seemed genuinely scared. I was used to the defeatist spirit of the people in Bârla, who had foreseen the end of the world many times before.

"What happened, Grigore?" I tried to find out details about the imminent cataclysm.

"The Russians shot Kennedy, boy." Before I could ask who Kennedy was, he whipped the horse, who started running like mad, as if he'd also just been touched by the gravity of the situation.

Before getting home, I didn't meet with anyone with whom to consult. The whole village was empty, as if people had already run to the mountains, and I found my dad with his head half gone into our radio, a huge box that sometimes gave off fragments of noisy and unintelligible news from Vocea Americii. A forbidden radio channel, which everyone listened to regardless.

"Quiet, quiet!" said mom closing the door with a key, though I'd said nothing. I glued a ear to the loudspeaker hoping I'd finally understand what had happened. Our radio functioned poorly because it was fed by an improvised source of power, made by dad: the famous and dangerous "bulrush" battery. It was made up of approximately the following: a glass jar in which he put a bent zinc plate, which surrounded a small sack, probably with coals, all of them floating in lots of sulphuric acid. Later on, the fully finished batteries that dad would test on his tongue came out. If it was good, it would pinch you if you put your taste buds on both ends at the same time.

President Kennedy's assassination was a clear sign, not only that the Americans had gone insane, but also that they'd never come to free us from the Russians. At night, I heard dad telling mom:

"Vili, poor man, still hoped they'd come... He said they were our only hope, and this Kennedy would have been the right man. It's all gone to shit now."

Smoking, Laura and Naphthalene

With Uncle Vili and Kennedy dead, us erased from the Americans' goodwill list, my folks went into a period of crisis. Dad was quiet and smoked a lot, mom sighed more often in the house, and we played desperately outside, and we all waited to leave "for good" to the city.

In the end I also started smoking. Dad would send me to the store to buy him some cheap unfiltered cigarettes. I don't even think filters had been invented yet. With a leu they'd give me two packs and three cigarettes. Coming home with Wolf, we lit our first cigarette which we smoked together, hidden behind a fence. We had to hold on to it, from the dizziness. But we liked it and repeated the experience, becoming confirmed smokers later on.

Along with the discovery of cigarettes, I also learned to be interested in girls. Or maybe the presence of a cigarette between my lips made me more attractive, more interesting. At that age the girls always made the first move. I had some memories from around eight or nine, with the daughter of some neighbors, older than me of course, who would open up my "spielhosen," playing curiously with my dick. She would tell me: "Let's pretend to be mommy and daddy" and search industriously through my pants. I was much lonelier in the role of the father.

With Laura, the daughter of the militiaman, it was otherwise. She'd say directly: "Let's go do naughty things." The "naughty things" started one day when we found ourselves alone at home.

"Let's hide together," she said.

"And who will look for us?" I asked.

"No one."

We went into the closet, a huge crate, and we sat on nicely folded sheets and blankets. We closed the door only enough for a bit of light to shine through, to feel our faces and vaguely see the clothes hanging from hangers over us. Lots of dresses, shirts, overcoats of her mother's, all soaked in overpowering perfumes, and a militiaman's uniform, with its rancid whiff of authority that so frightened me. The heavy smell of naphthalene floated over all of this, dominated that closet of my first erotic experiences.

Laura would unbutton my pants and go there with a hand that had begun to lose its innocence. We took our underwear down to our ankles.

"You do what I'm doing," she'd always say, convinced that someone who wanted to become a clown had to know how to imitate well. I'd open the closet's door wider to see what was hiding between her legs better. The word "birdie" didn't satisfy me at all. In my head I named it crack, though I didn't exactly use this word. I felt it was a dangerous entrance not only into a woman but into the mystery from whence we come. A dangerous labyrinth, so I treaded carefully there with my fingers, as if I were afraid not to open a black hole that would suck me in greedily. Anyway, Laura liked it a lot.

Sometimes she made me imagine what might hide behind our impatient children's "naughty things." She confused me with her tiny breasts and the hair that started growing in places where I was still bare-skinned. We were totally uninhibited, and she succeeded in creating erections that amazed me and which neither of us knew what to do with.

Once she got completely naked, opened up her legs and asked me to climb on top of her. We strained and struggled ignorantly, one over the other, until her father's uniform fell on us, scaring us with its shoulder badges and its smell of a stern man, who sweats heavily in his rages. One of the white granules went right in there, between her legs, and for a long time afterward I associated the weird smell of the "crack" with that of naphthalene balls.

We never kissed and it never went through our head. We never spoke about what was happening in the closet. We were like two whelps who smelled out each other's organs. We mimed sex instinctively, exercised the movements of togetherness like two impatient mimes. Laura was very free and good-hearted, so she decided to include a cousin of hers in our game. They hid by turns, me spending all my time in the naphthalene closet. This is how the idiot idea that girls were all about the same, and if you want to do something between their legs you only have to stay alone with them pretending that you're playing hide and go seek, got into my head.

Moving Out

In 1965, the year when we moved to Bistriţa, Gheor-ghiu-Dej died too. I saw his burial on TV, and that was the first time that I came in contact with that new box with moving images. The school was able to buy the first TV in the area, or more exactly to receive one in exchange for a large quantity of old clothes that teachers and students had collected over the course of several months. The auditorium was filled to the brim. People were quiet but delighted for two reasons: they were watching TV for the first time and they could assist in the burial of the man they detested—live. Death alone remained the same, impartial with everyone like a divine law. Our leaders being not elected but installed, seemed eternal beings, deified like pharaohs. Their deaths, totally non-cyclical events, were awaited passionately and impa-tiently by those who built pyramids of hate for them or dug them sacrificial canals with guns at their temples.

I was on the verge of moving away from Bistriţa for about two months, as if I were waiting for some kind of passport. We weren't going to move definitively or temporarily. No one had yet given the signal for the huge migration of villagers to cities. Industry, the magical word of triumphalist communism, which had already begun to raise its wings, was still in its plucked turkey phase.

Bistriţa was a small town of about twenty thousand people, somewhat more than it had had six hundred years earlier, when Germans emigrating from Saxony built it after the model of Medieval fortified strongholds. Back then they had to defend against Asian and Turkish invasions. Now it was a mixed town, with Romanians, Hungarians and Jews added to its population, all of whom could no longer defend against the new invasion, much more tenacious and perverse. No one could raise defensive walls anymore, moats, battlements against the communism that spread everywhere like a plague.

The Germans, after living, resisting and building there for centuries, gave up and wanted nothing but to return to the place their ancestors had left. Places long erased from their memories, where the dialects they still spoke had disappeared in the Middle Ages. Living among them, I assisted in their sad and apparently peaceful retreat.

Neighbors, childhood friends, classmates, lovers were leaving one after another, leaving behind an emptiness that was hard to fill. Homes that were fast falling to ruins, villages and towns that were losing a part of their identity, churches, cathedrals, synagogues into which God had gone with a drowsiness from which he couldn't be awakened. It seemed unfair to me for them to leave, and as I grew up, even more unfair for us to remain there without an escape, in a place where, after all, we all belonged. Only the sweet potatoes of the Roșu family continued to grow every year, more and more wild.

Mom didn't pack anything, like the others, though we could have moved any day. There wasn't much to pack anyway and if something had come up, like some truck coming to Șieu on business, she would have thrown everything into a crate or some beds that we'd have tied at the edges. I spent the last month there from morning till evening patrolling between the tavern and a kind of village store that sold everything. I was waiting for the truck that would come take us away from there already.

Since I was young, I hated the transit network, those dreadful, torturous periods that stretch like a smoky bridge between decisions and actions. As we waited to leave, Șieu's dimensions grew smaller by the day, like a consumed dream, and Bistrița grew, enlarging its streets, multiplying its stores and cinemas, and the cathedral downtown swelled up in my head like a medieval donut.

If I saw a truck passing on the dusty road, I would lie desperately in the middle, frightening the drivers who I asked whether they could take us to Bistriţa. When they found out we were talking about two beds, a closet and four chairs, they got scared and left immediately. One day, I convinced one of them who had brought beer to the bar that the transport was light, not counting one of the beds, the closet and my sister, who was tiny anyway. I showed him where we lived and he told me to climb to the cabin, because he was in a hurry. I preferred to remain attached to the stairs like a gangster. Happy beyond measure, I lit a cigarette that I stuck between my lips and I perched myself there so the whole village could see me. When I entered the yard, I threw the butt and cried to my mom, who was washing the clothes:

"I'm done, mom. Pack up, 'cause we're moving!"

Dad was fishing and when he came, everything was in mom's crate and two wool beds. My sister had a single doll, and I had a screwed-up weapon with a bow which threw an arrow with a suction cup that no longer stuck to anything. When I left, I didn't look back. I forced myself this time out of a kind of superstition that I made up on the spot, telling myself that if I was weak and looked back, I'd return to live in that place for the rest of my life. It was like a defensive reflex, something instinctive, which I'd repeat later whenever I moved from one place to another.

Mom and my sister went into the cabin of the track, dad followed us on his motorcycle, drowning in a cloud of dust, and I hide myself in that closet. Mom stretched out a rope there where she hanged wet clothes, and dad threw behind some fish caught that day. Our shirts, socks and underwear waved in the wind like flags in retreat. Adios, Șieu!

If I had had someone to talk to and something to say, my voice would have drowned for sure. I opened the door to our only closet and went into it. I stayed crouched inside it, overwhelmed by emotions that were crushing my head and the rattling of the logs that made up the foremost décor of my childhood. After we passed the last bend in the village, I left the closet and looked calmly behind.

The Maidan

We arrived in Bistrița around noon. The clothes washed in Șieu had dried, and dad's fish were beginning to smell. It never crossed my mind to ask them where we'd stay. Bistrița was an old town where nothing had been built since before the last world war. Ionică, a cousin of mom's, lived alone in a house in Decebal, a neighborhood close to downtown, and had agreed to rent a room with access to a kitchen and the toilet in the yard. The whole house was in a state of ruin that no one bothered to remedy after his parents' death. Only the yard and orchard out back showed any sign of being cared for. We were moved in three moves; mom took out a pot and fried the dish, our first meal at the new home.

In the afternoon I went outside, curious to explore the area where I'd spend the next years or maybe the rest of my life. In front of our row of houses a huge meadow stretched, its grass cut short by the groups of geese and ducks that nibbled it at their leisure, like in the country. Beyond the uncemented road was the town's big square, then the Liviu Rebreanu High School, a mixed Romanian-German school, with lots of sports fields, yards and imposing buildings erected in the days of the Austro-Hungarians. That's where the old Medieval town started, dominating the downtown area with the steeple of the huge cathedral, its massive stone houses, glued, leaning on one another, with small streets and passages so narrow that the neighbors could hold each other's hands from one window to another.

If you were curious and went through the big, arched gates, you discovered another world. From the German doorknobs, unchanged for hundreds of years, still in working order, to the manual boots that pumped water through a canalization that had undergone few changes, causing a slow dampening that soaked the walls over the course of centuries. In the spring, when the sun was shining and you went into one of the old yards, you felt the smell of this secular humidity, deposited in layers of mold and history.

It was around the end of July, on a Saturday, and the maidan in front of the house where we had just moved was full of colorful stalls where a bunch of people were strolling. The largest human gathering I'd seen till then, several hundreds. My folks gave me a leu to get an ice cream and I started to walk through that fair of wonders situated right underneath our window. Barracks where you could shoot with guns or arrows, stalls where you threw circles, balls, pellets, fortune tellers, coffee, coals, bean-pods, pendulums that you started and you never had to return to again, deceiving mirrors. Charlatans galore, a man with three arms, a man without arms, the snake-woman, a cyclops himself, the child without joints, and other rare malformations exhibited for a surcharge in tents painted grotesquely. A policeman patrolled nervously, his cane in his hand. A gypsy winked at me with her only eye, and told me:

"If this guy let me read his palm, I'd plant terror into him. You, boy, on the other hand, I'd guess your fate for more or less nothing. You have lots written on your forehead, you darling!"

I don't know what came over me, but I threw the little money I had left into her lap, dying from curiosity to find out how my new life would go. She took me by the hand and said something like:

"You'll soon have problems in your head, then luck and again problems and again luck. Even so, always luck in the end. This is what matters. When all's said and done, you'll trip a bit."

I didn't even take two steps and I fell, tripped from behind by someone's leg. I awoke with my face in the grass full of goose shit and discarded ice cream. When I tried to get up, I saw four boys around me in a circle, looking at me from above, furious.

"Who sent you here?" the biggest one asked me, a tall, muscular redhead of about 15.

"No one sent me," I answered. "I came alone."

"If you're lying, you'll pay for it! I know the folks by the bridge sent you to spy on us."

"I just moved to that house," I told them, showing them Ionică's house. This disconcerted them and they suddenly looked differently at me.

"Why didn't you say so, kid? We might have broken one of your ribs by mistake. So you say you live in our neighborhood?" I nodded my head and the guy who seemed to be their boss stretched out his hand to me and I got up. "I'm Costea," he said, "the boss of the Hrube gang. These two are my brothers, Petre and Mircea, the fat one is Radu, she's Gina and she's a girl, though she doesn't seem like one. We all have passwords, but we don't share them with anyone."

I tell them my name and add, disconcertedly, that I've never had a password.

"We'll find you one if you deserve it and you want to be with us."

That's how I got into the gang in Hrube on the first day, one of the two rival gangs that disputed their neighborhoods territorially, Hrube and Next to the Bridge. In Hrube there was a big square, that's where the circus would come and set up the paradise of all kinds of circus performers. Next to the Bridge was situated around the river, the place where we bathed and where the stadium and town park were. I don't know where this medieval rivalry of theirs came from, which would consume a good chunk of our spare time, which we might call just about all the time at our disposal back then.

Both neighborhoods belonged to the former Romanian settlements situated outside the old walls of the German town, communities that rivaled one another historically.

My new friends asked me what I could do. Meaning if I could do something concretely, like fighting with my fists or something else, if I knew how to use a slingshot or bow, if I could leave my house at night, and what amazed me most, if I could perform on any instrument. I told them I'm a master of the slingshot and bow, but that I hadn't yet decided on any instrument. Radu stretched out his slingshot doubtfully; I loaded a rock, and one of the few public bulbs remaining in the neighborhood was pulverized under the passing glances of the policeman who was looking for us, knocking his cane against his palm. After that they started opening up to me and I found out that they were my neighbors.

I spent the following years outside, with them, that street being more of a home to me that the single room where we were all crowded. Plus the kitchen where I learned while mom was cooking, supervising me with a large wooden spoon in her hand, ready to knock my head if my eyes wandered away from the book pages. It was horribly difficult to concentrate, knowing that outside, in the street, so much was happening without me. The books and all the knowledge in them smelled of fried food. I think I had created a kind of conditional reflex for myself in that kitchen, feeling hungry and nauseated at the same time whenever I opened a schoolbook. The future didn't frighten me at all, no matter how much mom tried to scare me with it. I envisioned it as a tiny mouse that ran quickly into a hole in the sky as soon as I thought about it. A very abstract mouse, of course, and I was the cat.

The Circus is Coming!

One August morning, not long after we moved, I had the revelation of a miracle. When I looked out the window, I saw an elephant. The first elephant of my life. I wiped my eyes, convinced I was having a vision in which the future was showing itself to me in its true form and gravity. A big tent had been pitched just in front of our house and about five, six people were pushing and pulling the huge animal, which seemed more real and even more scared than me. I went out; our maidan was unrecognizable.

Overnight, the circus had come. Dozens of people were hastily erecting a huge canvas cupola on big polls, sustained by ropes, levers and pulleys. An itinerant menagerie was in the process of being installed right under our window. Lots of wagons on wheels, some huge cages with grating that they were putting down into squares like the Americans from the wild west when they were attacked by Indians. Two tigers, two lions, three monkeys, some ponies, a boa, a seal, two native pelicans, molting wolves, exotic birds, guinea fowls, plus the elephant from the tent and a zebra with pretty faded stripes.

Radu, the pork butchers' son, who lived two houses away from me, was already outside and was staring at the whole agitation while biting through a log-thick piece of salami. His parents worked at a sausage factory, were also fat, and their house was full of different salamis put out to dry in the most unexpected places. He was the only fat boy in the city and you couldn't call him anything but "The Fat Kid." Only he got angry when you called him that when he ate. And he ate often. Once, he beat the hell out of a kid who was much bigger than him, using a piece of salami as a stick.

"These folks with the circus come every year," he told me. "This time they brought the whole jungle with them. It'll smell really bad."

The elephant stank worst of all, as if the smell in animals was proportional to their size, and it was parked right underneath our window. Some animals were used for training purposes, others simply belonged to the menagerie and whoever wanted to see them had to pay. If I ignored the stench, we were very privileged for our location, and after several days we seemed to be a part of the itinerant circus, freely going wherever we wished.

For two weeks the life of our gang revolved around the circus. We were present at every representation, going underneath the canvas. My desire to become a clown came back and I practiced various numbers and gags by mistake, without stirring too much amusement around me. The circus, despite the communism that had changed everything that moved in the country, remained the same. The tightrope walk was still done on the tightrope, the trapeze jumpers flew, trying to catch the same bars with their hands, while underneath them nets were being put down to catch those who messed up. The hopeless, free-falling phase hadn't begun yet in the emptiness that the system was perversely creating around us, growing like a deadly cavity.

The only thing I didn't like was the animals' training. I hated seeing strong lions subdued like cats forced to do meaningless things. The elephant under my window was transformed into the most pitiful creature. It was crying and no one observed this. It was crying naturally, and it seemed to me the most fantastic thing that an animal was doing in the circus arena. Evening after evening, when it had to climb a drum and stand there on a leg like a stupid loser forced to prostitute itself before our wild fair, it would change its facial expression completely. Its eyes would become sad and it would cry with white, huge tears, which fell down its cheeks and trunk. I was convinced that that elephant had a soul that was in the process of falling apart.

When I attracted the others' attention toward this, they laughed in disbelief and my folks looked strangely at me. Only mom reacted differently, telling me that once, when she was small and getting close to puberty, she saw a sheep that had become depressive and weepy after grandpa decided to cut it up for Easter, and which had committed suicide by jumping into a ravine.

I started studying the elephant closely, looking at it for hours on end from the window. At one point it started to feel my presence and greeted me with its trunk.

Close to the menagerie the family of the trapeze jumpers lived. The only person who had observed the real tears of the elephant was the daughter of the circus performers. Her name was Nora and I had a relationship with her from the very beginning, ever since our glances first met one another. That's when I started to believe in love at first sight, or at least in that kind of connection that doesn't appear at all if it doesn't appear at the very beginning.

Nora and Rajah's Tears

It was in a morning in which I had gone, as usual, under the circus' canvas, and I was following the training of the circus performers from a corner. The trapeze jumpers were training their daughter every day like a future gladiator that would soon fight in the arena for life or death. I could hear her bones crackling when her father would bend her spine until her nape was touching her ankles. That's how I think she saw me for the first time, glancing toward me obliquely, like a tableau awkwardly set on the wall. Then she looked at me for a long time, until her father slapped her and began to bend her again like a doll.

She seemed smaller than me. She was thin, skinny and tortured, with budding breasts and feminine forms like Olympic gymnasts. She had unusually large bags under her eyes for a child, and on her neck were two swollen veins that made you believe that in her chest there was a pressure too great for her to endure. She seemed to train somehow on the inside even when she didn't move. I followed her very attentively several days in a row. Clenching her teeth whenever she went on the wire, making incredible jumps on the land or catapulted by a trampoline at the end of which her mother was jumping, throwing her in the air like a cat. She would land on the shoulders of her father, who was never pleased. She didn't seem happy at all to do what she was doing and it seemed to me that I was assisting a sort of training. Her parents didn't whip her, but they didn't give her sugar cubes either. Or at least a warm and grateful smile, like my mother's when I got a crappy passing grade in math, a subject that was my own difficult wire walk.

After training, I saw her in front of the elephant. She was eating a sandwich with a hand, and with the other she was caressing it, and when I got close to her she told me straight:

"If you really like to stare at me so much, I want you to show me your house. I haven't seen a real house since I was small."

"How old are you?" I asked her. The elephant was following us with its glance from overhead, like a careful umpire.

"I'm older than you, even though I don't seem it. I'm fifteen."

I was getting close to fourteen, and the elephant, as I would find out from her, was 45 and was named

Rajah. A veteran who had caroled throughout Europe, and a true survivor of the second world war. In 1944, the train it was transported in was bombed and derailed somewhere in Transylvania. Rajah escaped alive, together with several lions and a zebra. The Germans were retreating, and the Russians who were marching forward with their tanks found themselves with the elephant racing like crazy toward the outskirts of a forest, followed by the two lions that had eaten the zebra in the meantime and were attacking people's sheep. It's rumored that the Russians stopped the attack, perplexed by the space they had gone into or by the possible tricks of the Romanian army, which mere months before had fought against the Soviets. Several tanks had reluctantly opened fire, but the animal escaped as if through a miracle with some wounds and holes in its huge ears. Hungry, the Russians ate everything, and the elephant might have ensured the nourishment of an entire division.

Toward the winter, when the first snow fell, he got off at the first village. Some peasants found him eating their hay in the barn and were convinced that it was a creature sent by God or one of those spirits in which their ancestors had believed long before Christianity. It was pulling three plows from behind.

I took Nora home and showed her our kitchen and the room we all stayed in. My folks weren't home and I let her look at all the walls, though there wasn't much to see. She seemed curious, as if she'd just gone into a strange museum. Our family pictures interested her. In one of them all four of us were together, and I was smiling awkwardly and unnaturally, a wry smirk. Dad had tried without success to show me how to smile when you're taking a professional picture. I was wearing an oversized suit, the sleeves of which my hands outgrew at only 15.

"In this picture you have a smile that's not yours. I don't even think you know how to laugh for real. This is why I like you." Then she paused, during which time I didn't know what to do, so I attempted a clown smile, some monkey business that I thought to do so as not to embarrass myself even more.

"Did you notice that the elephant cries?" I asked her.

"He's crying more and more. Sometimes I hear him in the night wailing loud."

I was glad that someone was finally confirming this. I felt like I was going insane with my worries about the elephant's depression, which only I seemed to see.

"I think he's even more tired of the circus than I am."

It seemed weird to me that this girl hated what she did so well. Look at me, suddenly face to face with someone from the circus, a future great acrobat that hated the world she lived in. A pretty confusing position for me, great admirer of the circus as an idea and way of life. I'd started, without noticing, to yearn for movement, for change, for the migrations that I foresaw in my life. This girl had already gotten tired of them, she wanted to wake up every morning in the same place, in a house without wheels. She even liked the crowded place we lived in. A room where you could hardly move because of the old furniture and the aggressive chairs you hit with every step.

She lay down on our only couch as if on a throne, and ordered me like a confident princess:

"Come and lie next to me. I won't eat you."

I lay by her mechanically, without expecting a second invitation. We were so crowded that I was sure that something weird would have to happen. She put my hand behind my shoulder and asked me to do the same. We were glued one to the other, and her feminine scent, a new supernatural smell, troubled me greatly. It was as if an angel had just wafted its perfumed wing by me. The only thing humanizing her in that moment was a hairpin that held her hair at the edge of her forehead, revealing more of it than it should have. That's how I always remember her. With those big, troubled eyes, the large forehead like a meadow that her hair, though it would have liked to, couldn't cover because of that ever-present hairpin which seemed stuck there for all eternity, passing through her black hair, through her skin, the bones of her head and her thoughts, which otherwise would have fallen apart.

"Do you know how to kiss?" she asked me. I nodded my head in the affirmative, as strongly as I could, as if my whole future life depended on it, and I waited to see what would happen. I stooped toward her, but our noses touched like two awkwardly placed hurdles. She passed her tongue over her lips and found my mouth with them. I stayed there like an idiot until she pinched my cheeks with her hand like a cherry that had to spit out its seed. My lips opened up and then I felt her wetness for real, her smell, breathing and tongue all going under my skin at the same time and making me dizzier than I had ever been, dizzier than when I was burning with fever in the winter, ruined by the worst tonsillitis. When we unglued each other, my voice abandoned me and I was left mute and red. Mom came in and I succeeded after a long pause in saying:

"She's the trapeze jumpers' daughter… she's also saying that the elephant cries."

Mom had no reaction. Surprisingly to me, she neither yelled at me nor stopped me from bringing her again to our place. The second day she left a dish with cookies on the table, to serve her if she came back.

"The circus people's daughter doesn't seem to eat three times a day," she added.

I only wanted to lie down again on that couch and continue where we had left off during that first kiss of my life. But Nora jumped to the cookies and didn't stop eating until there were only two or three, which she stuffed into a pocket. I had to accompany her to the menagerie, though I wasn't in the mood for the elephant, where she fed the animal with mom's cookies. It was a transparent relationship between them, because when Nora appeared, Rajah began waving his ears like atrophied wings. He would smell her gratefully with his trunk, swaying happily on a leg and then another like a silly fool who just got his toy back. After he vacuumed the cookies, he lay down on his knees in front of us and Nora climbed up on his head in two moves.

"Come on, you climb too, what are you waiting for? He's doing it only for us and he's doing it for fun."

I climbed fearfully and mounted the elephant's back, behind her. He got up slowly with us, as if we weren't even there and he wanted to leave. Only then did I notice the thick wire that one of his legs was tied to. He began shaking it apathetically like a convict who hasn't lost his last hopes yet.

I was glued to Nora and, having nowhere to rest my arms, I held her by the chest. I felt her every rib like bony claps and above them, her tiny and hard breasts, almost bony, from which her nipples jutted stiffly and tickled the bottom of my palms like unquiet, miniature trunks. I could feel her scent in my nostrils and unconsciously began to chew on one of her ears, which had gotten into my mouth.

Nora turned around with her face toward me, surrounded me with her legs and gave me my first lesson in kissing, long and convincing. All of these things happening at once became bigger and more powerful than the elephant under us, which was melting little by little. I don't know how long we stayed perched there on his neck, but I know that in that evening all women began for me with Nora's smell, breasts, lips and closed eyes.

I couldn't sleep until close to morning. I stared out the window toward the circus in front of the house, which seen in the moonlight seemed suddenly smaller, part of the eternally dusty landscape around us. I could hear the chain tied to Rajah's leg clattering helplessly, and it seemed unfair that an animal so strong, the largest land animal, should stay helplessly condemned in a menagerie.

I suddenly intuited, perceived everything with a part of myself that I didn't know existed, a kind of new, unbaked organ, like a transplant that had yet to find its place in my mind and body. I vaguely felt that something would happen soon with me, and a strange restlessness, the first restlessness of my life, invaded me like muddy, oozing water. I had forgotten Şieu and my short anterior life there that was going faster and faster away from me, like a landscape seen from a train that's going at the speed of sound.

In the days that followed, I did nothing but spy on Nora, smelling her like a cat in heat that strolls dizzily, sleepwalking on roofs. All my priorities had changed, like the pawns on a chess table that start to move alone amongst each other until you no longer know what color you're playing against.

I was meeting more and more rarely with the guys in the gang; archery, escapades through the woods and fishing mattered less and less to me. In the day, I was following the acrobats' exercises, on the prowl to spy the moment when Nora's parent would train her,

torturing her tiny body in all sorts of ways. It was painful to watch her. She didn't seem happier than Rajah,
but I couldn't take my eyes off her. She knew I was there
and that I was following her stealthily.

I waited for the coming of the evenings when the
circus show that I knew by heart would start. That's
when I met with Nora and we would go to the back
of the yard, where we stretched our bodies on the dry
hay gathered into a haystack that grew wider with each
passing day. Nora would open up my trousers and play
differently than the policeman's daughter from Șieu.
It was no longer that game of hide and go seek among
clothes smelling of naphthalene. Sometimes I grew
unexpectedly and grew hard in her hand, and then all
my troubles were gathered there in that excrescence. A
dangerous refuge that I hadn't known about until then.
She would raise her skirt and place my hand in that
place that I knew, but which now vibrated and moved
and grew wet like a living being. She didn't wear underwear, and in one of those last evenings, she said to me:

"When I come next year, you'll go inside me. You're
not ready for that yet."

It didn't go through my head to contradict her or
ask her something idiotic. It was obvious that she was
right, and I hadn't even the slightest trace of masculine
pride then. It grew in me much later, along with my
mustache, beard, acne and useless and painful erections
that I didn't know what to do with. Then, I wanted
to learn the mysteries of the world one by one, and

my instincts still warred in silence in the menagerie of my mind.

The second day it was Sunday, the circus was resting, and Nora came nicely dressed on the neighborhood's lawn where I played with the boys. I presented her like a minor celebrity, but she didn't seem interested in the others' company. She didn't want and I don't think she knew how to play like a normal kid. She was different from the rest of us. She was neither a kid nor an adult, neither a girl nor a woman.

"I want to go on the town to eat some ice cream," she said as she showed me a five lei bill, which was enough for other debaucheries as well. I left the others, who definitely envied me; I put on my Sunday pants and shoes and told my folks that I'm going to church. Church? This was too much, I had never gone like that to church, out of nowhere.

"The circus performers' daughter wants to." I said it to feel less guilty somehow. Closeness to God always made me feel uncomfortable in my own shoes, especially when I lied. Mom sometimes made us pray at night before going to sleep and I knew that she would have wanted us kids to be somewhat more religious. That is, to have more fear of the Lord, since at the end of the day it was all about fear and I didn't really like this.

On the way, I showed Nora the high school where I'd go in the fall. I had no idea what it looked like inside, but on the outside it was a sumptuous, massive, imposing building. Built by the Germans during the days of the Empire, it transmitted a kind of heavy guarantee of the continuity of a world that would continue in time indifferent to the times.

We got to the old, Medieval part of the city and went into a café. I bought two chocolate ice creams that I licked quietly at a table outside, watching nicely dressed people who were going to their respective churches down the main road. The closest one was the German cathedral, where the heavy sound of an organ could be heard. Nora wanted to go inside. I wondered at the way that she made the sign of the cross and sat down on a pew as if she went there for a serious reason. Then she started to pray, and I wanted to tell her that this wasn't an Orthodox church, but I abstained. If mom prayed on Sunday in the kitchen, why shouldn't an Orthodox pray in an evangelical church?

My folks never went to church, out of fear of being seen and turned over. If they found out that they were churchgoers, they could lose their teaching jobs. Atheism had become basically a subject taught in schools, but no one really took disbelief seriously, just as people didn't really care for belief either.

The organ began sounding a strong hymn, everyone got up on their feet and began to sing in German. Our stomachs and chests went into a strange and disturbing vibration, like resonating boxes. As if faith were perched right there, in our stomachs, without our knowledge. I know we felt the same thing because Nora put her hand on her chest, a misplaced eardrum whose vibrations had to be stopped, and she stared at me like a person who's going into a trance. I almost pulled her out of there, and when we got to the park she asked me very seriously:

"Do you believe in God and in the Resurrection?" It seemed an idiotic question, without realizing that it was the first time in my short life that someone asked me something so direct and complicated, for which I had no answer at hand.

"I have no idea." I preferred to take her to the kiosk in the park, where the town's fanfare was singing the same waltzes and marches that didn't make anything vibrate in us.

"This evening is our last show. Tomorrow we're packing up and leaving."

I hadn't thought until then about her leaving. I felt an emptiness in my stomach, in the same place where the cathedral's organ had vibrated, and this reinforced the feeling that my belly was more than the place where food went. We walked through the park in silence. Nora tried several times to take my hand, but it seemed weird that two kids should walk hand in hand in the town park where everyone could see us. But it didn't seem at all wrong to do what we would do in the haystack. Maybe that evening, our last evening, we'd take it further, though I had no idea how far a guy and girl could go. It was clear to me that we'd go as far as Nora wanted.

"We'll see each other next year. In the meantime, I'll write you."

"And where should I send you my answers?"

"I don't know. Itinerant circuses don't have addresses."

The Wedding on the Elephant's Back

I got home looking like a rained-on turkey hen and mom asked me how the meeting with divinity went. After I ate, I went down to the cellar and filched a cherry brandy bottle, about two years old, full of sour cherries. Suddenly the idea came to me to celebrate her and the circus' departure as we should, like grown-ups. The men would say that cherry brandy was a weak drink, for women and children. I took two cigarettes from my father's pack and put two glasses and some nut cookies in my pocket. I waited for her in the back of the orchard, rubbing the cigarette between my fingers. She brought me a picture of hers in a school uniform, with a braid in her hair and long tresses, from when she was around 9.

"When I was small, they sent me to school for several years. Maybe this fall they'll send me again."

I tried to fill the glasses with the little alcohol that remained in the bottle and toasted it like a veritable man.

"To this summer and the year that is to come!" I lit a cigarette, took a deep, manly drag into my chest, and handed it to her. She didn't smoke, but she took a small drag, enough to choke. We clinked our glasses, drank to the bottom, then coughed and shook. It was stronger than we expected, and when I tried to refill the glasses only sour cherries fell out. We spat their seeds while a pleasant drowsiness took over our bodies and flesh. Nora already had her hand down my pants, which recognized her with everything in them. She took it out and the movements of her hands had something desperate, frenetic this time, and I answered differently. She kissed me for the first time on the neck, drawn out, then on the ear, and my neck and ear recognized her immediately. I don't know how far we went, because drunk as we were, we fell asleep in each other's arms.

When we got up, there was a big full moon over us, such as I'd never seen before. Nora was almost naked and had goosebumps. Fall was coming and the hoar frost had settled already on the shiny skin of the plums in the trees. I don't think my pants had gotten wet because of her. I still vaguely had in my mind the feeling of the weird outbreak that dizzied and troubled me worse than the brandy. It was quiet and late, the circus show had finished long before and no one was looking for us.

During summer vacation I was exempted from nagging. My folks wanted to see us outside as much as possible, so they could enjoy some intimacy before the start of the schoolyear and the cold.

"Let's go see Rajah," I told them. We put on our clothes and left through the yard, still dizzy. When we got to the elephant, I still had the brandy bottle in my hand. He smelled it with his trunk and made a loud sound that broke the peace around us. Everyone had gone to sleep, the lights were off at my house, my folks were sleeping peacefully knowing that I was somewhere outside, in a world where nothing bad could happen to me.

The clock on the tower sounded the midnight bell and Nora, the elephant and I seemed the only beings in the world who were awake. Rajah continued to pull on the bottle, so I poured some cherries into my palm, which he took into his mouth before greedily gobbling up everything that was left. I had to shake the bottle in front of him to convince him that it was empty. He sat down on his knees so we could climb him.

"You go first," Nora said.

I climbed his neck, and from there I saw her looking for something in a box. Just after she mounted in front of me did I understand that she'd found the key of the lock that locked the elephant's chain. She opened it. He left with us like a bullet, and we had to stick to his body so as not to hit our heads against the tent's bars over our heads. We went exactly in front of our window, through which, illumined by the moon, I saw my folks sleeping quietly. Dad, like always, with his night-cap on and the cotton in his ears to avoid the current, and mom next to him, her blanket up to her ears, and my sister half fallen off the bed. From there Rajah made directly for the town.

Riding an elephant, if it's not running, is easier than riding a horse. It's like having the whole earth underneath you, dried and cracked like after a drought. You see the world from higher up, more grandiosely. Only that you also see it more frightened. At least in the beginning, until you get used to it and understand that nothing can happen to you while you find yourself up there, where you're untouched, truly outside the world, of the rules and of dogs that bark but can't bite you. Plus that you can't do anything about it, you can't go against anything. You're defended at that altitude from the dangers below you, but it's all left to fate when you think about how much can happen over your head.

Rajah didn't have a harness and even if he did, who knew how to drive an elephant? Jumping off it was out of the question, because we would have broken our legs and been eaten by the stray dogs that seemed to have lost their minds. And beyond everything, who could have guaranteed us that we would ever again ride a gentle elephant, drunk on cherry brandy? You also have the advantage of seeing everything double, because of its enormous head's swaying, which leads your eye over the landscape slowly and sideways, until you understand it better.

The carriages with gypsies on the maidan were the first things we came across. The women, in their colorful dresses, were heating something on an almost dead fire, around which men with stuffy mustaches dozed off, their pipes lit in their mouths. Lots of kids were hidden among rags and skinny horses that slept on their legs.

The dogs ran toward Rajah, who stopped in front of the gypsies as if they were a mandatory stop. With his trunk, he greeted these ancient descendants of India, whose ancestral memory perhaps had not forgotten the majestic image of the king of the jungle, symbolic in their culture.

They rose on their feet one by one, elbowing each other, slowly awaking those who were asleep. They seemed visited by a supernatural vision that sought them from somewhere in time. They said nothing, which for them was a grand performance, a true circus trick. Several of the old ones sat on their knees, and their confusion would have been much worse had they not seen us two, such native figures hanging on the elephant's neck.

Rajah was surrounded by a pack of hardened dogs who calmed down and disappeared only after one of them was thrown into the air by the elephant's leg, and another, picked up by the trunk and held over our heads, was made to fall like a rock.

It was clear that we had nothing to be afraid of. The whole group of gypsies was at our feet. An old woman kindled the fire with a stick, and it came back like a living thing. They all made way for a blackish, dry man who was wearing the longest mustache in the world under a hooked nose, thin as a blade. At his waist he had a wide girdle in which old coins were encrusted. When he started to talk, his golden teeth started sparkling through his dense mustache. I don't know what he said, because he spoke Roma, but Nora nodded as if she understood what he was saying, and everything seemed normal to me, even though it had never gone through my mind before that that she might have gypsy blood.

Then the boss, because it was clear that he was their ringleader, let his head fall back and, his eyes closed, began to monotonously hum a melody that didn't seem of this world. Someone was accompanying him from a carriage on an instrument with sounds that I wasn't used to. Rajah seemed just as hypnotized as myself and started to wave his ears and raise his trunk. He lay on his knees until we got to the level of the boss, who stopped singing, took a pipe from his girdle and lit it. After he took a couple of drags, he handed it to me. I took deep drags into my chest several times and, in spite of myself, started to cough. It didn't seem to be tobacco. A weird dizziness took hold of me, and after several moments, it seemed to me that that instrument had moved directly into my ears. I would have wanted to know what was in the pipe, because its blue smoke went deep not into my chest but into my head, coloring my thoughts, swelling them up like soap balloons.

Everything that happened that night remained in my mind like a dense dust scattered somewhere on the edge between dream and reality. Later, it would deposit itself, now on one side, now on another, of that arbitrary that we draw sometimes in the midst of the madness in which we live.

Nora also took several drags of the pipe and glanced at me over her shoulder with eyes I didn't know. I wouldn't escape that look for a long time, though I understood nothing of it then. They all started singing, sometimes more cheerful, rhythmic, and I saw them swaying as if through a dense cotton candy fog. I was about to faint. The boss put our hands together and we found ourselves with two crowns on our heads, perhaps of gold, which made us unrecognizable to one another. I felt so heavy that I could hardly move my eyes, but I was happy, and the only perception that mattered to me was Nora's smell, which took me over. We lay glued to one another, and I felt her from her soles to the top of her head, warm, molded after me as if she had grown there. After a while, Rajah got up with us; we looked like stunned humps, grown directly on his spine, and he slowly started toward the marketplace. We left the gypsies behind, dancing and singing, but their sounds followed us for a good amount of time, like a cloud of flies.

"What happened?" I asked her without a hint of curiosity. Nora was quiet for a while, and when I didn't hear any answer, she whispered in my ear:

"I think they married us according to their law."

"Are you sure, or do you just think that?"

"I think it."

We were both quiet, like children who, playing mommy-and-daddy, suddenly find themselves wearing clothes that are too large for them. Neither of us laughed.

We took the road toward the marketplace, where three carriages loaded with wooden logs from the woods stopped us in our path. They were smugglers and poachers from the Bargau villages, who lived at the edge of the mountains and laws. They circulated only at night and brought illegal firewood to the cities for the winter and venison. Dad wanted to buy something like that too. The horses, beautiful and well cared for, rose up on their hind legs scared, then galloped away, waking up their masters who were dozing off on jacks, always at the utmost limit of drunkenness from the plum brandy. I knew they wouldn't make a racket, like people who are born with a chip on their shoulder.

In the square there was a bunch of cabbage, cared for by a Romanian from the South who slept on a mat. Rajah found a large nob and started to chew on it hungrily. Then another. All you could hear was his munching. Although we were waking up from our drunkenness, we were still dizzy, fascinated and stayed silent instinctively, out of fear to not spread that state of being, as we didn't know what it would bring with it.

The man guarding the cabbage got scared, took a bat into his hand and he hastened to hit Rajah, as if he were an ordinary ox. A poor peasant who'd carried his goods from afar, so poor that he didn't care whether a cow or an elephant plundered him. He had to defend himself. When he hit his trunk, Rajah snatched the bat angrily.

"To hell with you, you damned shapeless monster! Phew, unclean devil, you've picked my cabbage? Jesus Christ, what's this about?!" He stood in front of the elephant, swearing at him helplessly.

"Rajah! Rajah! Don't hit him!" yelled Nora pleadingly, as if she were yelling at a cheeky cat. "What's the matter with you, man, to hit him? We're at a circus and we have authorization, do you understand, authorization. We train him at night. Leave him the hell alone, 'cause you don't live in two cabbage heads! He can squash you like a fly!"

For the first time I realized that Nora had another accent, like those in the South, or better said that she didn't have our accent. Rajah threw the bat with disgust, took another cabbage, turned around and left.

"Where are we going?" I asked, come out of my silence.

"Wherever he takes us."

But Rajah didn't go toward the circus. We didn't meet other people. The town seemed, if not dead, at least in a coma. We went by the high school, then took a narrow way that led directly downtown. It was like someone was whispering every shortcut into his ear. The passages were used in the Middle Ages for the evacuation of the town in case of an invasion. They were so narrow that Rajah barely fit; he rubbed against walls, and our heads touched the clothes put out to dry between houses. Through the windows we could see people sleeping, and cats were roughing it into the windows. He passed in front of the cathedral, careless of its grandeur. About four centuries before, when the Turks had invaded Transylvania, they'd gone into the city on two elephants in front and burned the holy place. I was quiet the whole time. I was digesting the same feelings with another mind. I had forgotten that we were on an elephant who, after all, had chosen to return by himself to the prison from which he no longer wanted to escape.

When I got back to the circus, there was a big ruckus. The trapeze jumpers, clowns, dad, mom, a policeman and other random observers were agitated in front of the menagerie, awakened from its slumber with all its creatures. When they saw us, they all grew petrified. It was a moment of silence, like when the Turks defiled the town. Rajah went guiltily into his tent, kneeled so we could get off, and if he could, he would have put his chain on his leg by himself.

The slaps Nora's parents gave her, on the other hand, rang in my ears like drums, and I jumped at them to hit them. Dad drew me aside, but he delayed the beating he proposed to give me. They carried Nora off after them like a sack, and I only had time to cry out to her:

"Write me, write me!"

Suddenly, it was quiet, and everyone left as if the show had ended. The last image I remember is that of the local policeman who, remaining alone with Rajah, struggled to write, with a chemical pencil that he softened in his mouth, a verbal process of what had occurred.

Disappearances

slept, or lay about, four days in a row, and when I
got up for good I decided to look out the window.
I knew that the circus had gone away with Nora,
the elephant and the gypsies. I tripped on the kitchen
threshold, and when I asked my mom for food I realized that my voice was growing thicker. I washed my
face and, staring at myself in the mirror, I noticed the
obvious shadow of a moustache over my upper lip. I had
grown several centimeters overnight; my hands and legs
had become longer and came out of my clothes like the
sticks of a scarecrow. Mom, who measured me a couple
of times near the threshold, thought and said resignedly:

"You'll wear your father's clothes for a while."

I went out to the square carrying a great emptiness after me, and I saw the boys playing soccer. They
stopped for a moment and asked me what team I
wanted to play for. From where, suddenly, so much

care for little me? I would soon find out that my reputation had grown much in the suburb and in the whole city. Not because of my physical height, but because of what had happened with Nora, who had grown like a donut while I was asleep.

Gossip and small talk went around with dizzying speed in those days, precisely because there were few telephones, and the ones that were around were definitely listened to. People were afraid to talk and came to make their list of prohibited things longer by themselves. They were more well-trained than the poor animals in the circus, who were fooled, at least; the animals gave reign to their speech and imaginations when they had to, unlike people. Gossip and mockery had become the sugar that people were allowed to have. Later, when I learned about Pavlov's experiments with his confused dog, I thought that we'd come to be both the dog and Pavlov at the same time. It was said—in whispers—that after the dog died, Pavlov continued to bring him food.

I thought for a while—and it still hasn't left me completely—that our mental health is tied to all these tiny and simple reflexes that accompany us day by day all our lives. Like ballasts caught by wings that learned to fly by themselves. If you let go of them, you lose them. Since that day, immediately after the circus left, I began to feel that beside my unusual physical growth, my mind was also growing. Only that the mind can grow in all directions, like roaring waters.

Anyhow, I'd made her pretty damn wide known. Who, apart from the Turks (of course), had gone through our poor town atop an elephant? What's more, the fucker—that is, me—had taken a girl with him, an acrobatic whore from the circus, and did as he pleased right there on the animal's neck. Everyone suddenly treated me with a respect that put me into a pleasant conundrum. As I'd come to learn, I had run away from home, had gone nuts for good; we took the world into our hands, two perverse kids—and the elephant was most handy. As if it wouldn't have been easier to run off on a train or bus.

In the end we hadn't broken any law, and even adults often ran away from home. Married people ran away from home too, women as much as men, the women with others' men and vice versa, and grown girls that had gone crazy from so much waiting and been kept at home ran away from their parents. It wasn't illegal to leave everything, with the condition that you'd stay in your world and not cry out like an ox. That is, that you wouldn't leave the country and you wouldn't complain that things were going badly in it. Because this meant betraying the fatherland, and condemnation for whoever did it.

Uncle Toader disappeared around then. A quiet man who visited us on a horse when I was living in Șieu. He only traveled this way: hunched on a beautiful saddle with lots of nails, leftover, he would say, by the Hungarian Hussars. I think he was the last true rider, and when he disappeared, he did it without the horse. His wife, much younger and poorer, would tell us that he'd thought about leaving to America for a long time. That's where he'd been born—of Ardelean parents who came back after making some money, like so many others. My folks got scared, because the traitor was a close relative.

No one had heard about him for the better of two years. His wife was already living with some guy from the neighboring village, who had moved into their home. She told everyone that she'd heard news from Uncle, who got to Chicago after passing the border in secret, an American city that he had no thought of leaving. I looked for a map of the world at school, and after I found America, I finally found the city of Chicago by a big lake—the place where Uncle Toader the Horseman lived. What a man, what courage!

One summer, a black Volga of the Securitate, with two Securitate officers in black, stopped before our house, frightening even the geese in the square. My folks hugged us in fear, though the Canal had been closed for a long time, and immediately started to get mentally ready for a long adieu.

"We're going to Bârla, to Toader's house," the older said, a frowning man who seemed born to know it all, and if he didn't know it, it didn't matter anyway. We all froze. "The kids can come too if you want to leave them at their grandparents,'" he added.

We traveled in deathly silence. On the bench in the back, staring at the sunken napes of the two Security officers, I was truly afraid for the first time—different from my routine horrors. In front of Toader's house there was lots of people, and the village's militiamen guarded the gate with a wolf.

"The kids will stay in the yard," said the boss. The entire yard was deeply dug into, turned upside down by the huge plough of a tractor. After a couple of minutes, I grew impatient and snuck imperceptibly into the summer kitchen, that semi-sheltered place where women cook in the summer and where all the fires start in the countryside. The furnace was outside, and under it there was a deep, nearly meter-long hole. Under it lay the remains of Uncle Toader. My folks identified him by his riding-boots, still intact, seemingly polished yesterday. Except for that, just white bones.

His wife with her lover, instead of running from home like normal people, had strangled Uncle Toader in his sleep, had hurriedly buried him under the furnace and thrown vitriol over him—lots of vitriol—so he'd disappear faster. She went on to cook the same rânțaș sauce and goulash above her husband. Love, then, may not just kill you; it can also cause you to kill. This idea shook me deeply, and since then I've been horrified of the word *vitriol* and of summer kitchens in the countryside.

The Gang from Hrube

After the circus left, all I could think about was Nora. She was always in front of my eyes, a cotton statue that grew and changed its forms like the clouds. I came back to the gang sad, burdened by heavy memories that I had decided to carry with me in silence. The square was a good refuge to keep my mind occupied. But I could hardly see the soccer ball that I kicked with my bony, quickly-grown legs, trippingly awkwardly like a drunken clown. They were all there: Radu "The Fat," the Podaru brothers whom we all feared, Pişta and his two smaller brothers, robotic twin aide-de-camps, ever-ready to serve him; Tase and his sister Gina, who stood by the gate and who was only able to convince us she was a girl and not a boy after a year, tellingly raising her skirt and shirt.

Emil was the cleverest among us, a born comedian, inventor of the "hit and run" division, future county-wide track champion and, afterward, a union leader. When I saw him again, after many years, he told me over a drink that if I stayed in Bistriţa two or three more days, he'd organize a strike in my honor. The Deac brothers, whose number I never found out exactly because only Dan and Rodica came regularly. They all studied in the German section, and they were in the gymnastics team. It was rumored that they might be Protestants, but I don't think they went to any church, and no one ever asked them to whom they prayed.

Creţu, the stamp-collector, whose voice changed the same week as mine, and who was thrown out of the chorus on the same day as me. We exchanged postal stamps, and we inspired each other to erase the stamps on them. A great gun-smith, he knew best how to make an almost-real pistol. He'd steal the metal tubes through which air was blown into truck-wheels, and he made pipes out of them, which he filled with sulfur from matches or even gunpowder taken from his father's hunting cartridges.

Gil the Businessman was there too, the strangest one among us, the kid who didn't know how to or want to play. He came around when you least expected it, mostly to show us that he was a decent enough neighbor and because he liked my sister, though he didn't quite know how to like her either.

George was also attracted to my sister—an older boy who would have known how to play but was too mature to get entangled with us. He came to the square only when she was there too, and then he'd offer to "organize" us; but we thought too highly of our mess, something unacceptable to him. Feeling flattered, my sister would have embraced George's "organization," to which Gil would have belonged had competition not upset him.

George had recently moved from Năsăud because he knew that physics and mathematics were better at our high school in Bistrița, though plums and apples ripened better over there. None of us could imagine that in the attic of George's house hid a real science-fiction lab, where he did all sorts of experiments. His mind grew straight, without useless windings, and he could solve any physics problem. He wanted to speak to me only when I told him that I'd like to build a miniature spaceship on the stairs. I don't know where I got the idea, and I confessed frankly to him that one night I had simply dreamed how such a spaceship is begun. He smiled thoughtfully and said I'm a "Bohemian." I looked in the dictionary and remember that the word's definition pleased me.

No one had found out anything about the episode with the gypsies, as if they'd never been there. When I asked them when the gypsies had left the square, they asked me: "What gypsies?" If they had known, many of them would have blamed their miserable sorceries.

Everyone knows that they lure and steal Romanian and Hungarian children, and even blond German kids with blue eyes, and turn them into gypsies. A theory that, if it could stand on its own two feet, would mean that you don't even have to be born a gypsy to get there. I never thought that they stole children, because they already had too many children. No one had any idea that they had married us too, and this thought, in all its grandeur, came into my head like a nail that I hammered myself. Later on, my grandfather would say about marriage that it has a "pressing heaviness."

The grandfather from Bârla had married for real, at the church, when he was 16, and grandma hadn't yet turned 15. When they started their conjugal life, they kept on being awkward, like a couple of neurotic children. She showed him her rag dolls, and he accidentally killed the cock in the yard when he shot an arrow to impress her. His father—my great-grandfather—broke his arrow, gave him his last beating and said: *Enough, playtime's over.*

I hadn't known my grandfather on my father's side because he'd died when dad was only three years old. He also married right after puberty, an age considered perfect back then for getting tied to another for eternity. His name was Machedon, and I came close to being called the same my entire life. It was grandma's idea. Mom wasn't against it; dad didn't insist; and for this reason grandma didn't quite convince mom. There was a bit of tension in the house when the winter made its way into our only room. Sometimes, when the silences grew too long, I thought that it might have been easier for me to be named Machedon, a lovely name in its way and one, moreover, which would have brought harmony to the family.

Grandpa Machedon must have been a proud man, like everyone from Năsăud. Even today they boast that among all the gathering of nations from the former Empire, they're the only ones given the charge of guarding the border, which they naturally built with their villages, soil, wives, children, animals and hounds in those eastern valleys. Maria Theresa (or maybe Franz Joseph, we're not sure anymore) allowed them to put together the famous Năsăud Border Patrol. But when the Great War broke out, I think their faith in them was all but shattered. Many left the village to fight for the emperor. Only two came back after four years. A blind man and Grandpa Machedon, a tail gunner on the front lines, untouched by bullets, shells, poisonous gas, foreign languages and customs, decorated and— most importantly—sane. I've always kept this in mind. Grandma said that I was very much like him. We only have a picture of him, in which, like all Transylvanian great-grandparents, he wears a uniform and the first moustache on the men's side of our family. He died a short while after the war from a simple pneumonia contracted after he had spent an entire day haymaking in the rain.

When I came back home at noon, mother was gathering a bunch of dirty clothes for washing. On top I saw the shirt I'd worn during my last night with Nora.

I took it and smelled it, breathing deeply, like a phthisis sufferer putting his oxygen mask on his face. Her smell invaded my every cell and made me drunk. My knees grew soft, and mom looked amazed at my face—the face of a morphine addict getting his fix. She pretended not to see me, but she understood everything, turned her back to me so I could hide the shirt that I'd come to smell daily.

For a while I hid it under the mattress, would smell it and grow excited in a tortured way, because I was almost never alone. Her olfactory remnants would stay impregnated there for months, until mom, seeing that I was going crazy, decided to throw it out. On that still-hot August day, she simply said to me:

"It's time you take a bath. You reek in a weird way, like a dog in heat. I'm giving you money to go to the communal bath."

I ate and went out to the square, where I convinced the Podaru brothers, Emil and Radu, that it's time to take a bath for good. No one had a bath with a bath-tub and shower at home. It was easier in the summer, because we'd wash ourselves in the yard with a hose and go bathing in the river.

The communal bath was in the city's park, and in the cold season there, we got rid of all the filth that deposited itself on our bodies in layers. It was a place where people socialized nude, exchanging gurgling reactions through the heavy steam of a stinking sauna beneath big, rusty, sprinkler-like showers connecting straight to the boilers of a damp hell. The water flowed continuously over men's drooping bellies, over their penises and dangling scrotums, which hung disgustingly like meaningless bells.

There were only two kinds of men there: the skinny, dry and tall ones like splintery Pinnochios, and the big-bellied ones who were on the brink of exploding. Here I realized that the size of the penis has nothing to do with the size of the body, and because I'd begun growing, I prayed to God to make mine bigger because I intuited that the bigger, the better.

We—the unfinished ones—stood in line to make our way into the world of the hairy, who knew everything about life. We tried to cover our growing organs with the same hands with which we tortured them as soon as we remained alone.

In a small town like ours, everything was well-hidden yet in plain view; everything was covered while being seen, everything was known. And life was a fake thing that walked naked down the street, and all the unfinished ones—if you asked them—went to bed with it.

"Come on, you fools, you come in here too," we were told every time, and we knew that it wouldn't be long before we'd go in somewhere, though we had no idea where.

"I know a hole where we can check out the women," said Emil.

With the women there were even more bellies, and the sagging breasts that looked like the carnal symbols of a disgraceful capitulation. A great disappointment for my eyes, which stared greedily through that first crack that connected me directly with the adult woman's unusual body. Until Emil's sister appeared in the foreground, covered in soap-bubbles like a wild Aphrodite—an 18-year-old girl whose fantastic form instantly erased all other visions from my mind. She seemed a moving statue, custom-made. I saw her a mere two meters away from me, her legs spread, and when she began washing herself slowly, lengthily and boldly, especially down there, her facial expression changed. She closed her eyes from pleasure and bit her lower lip. It even seemed that she was grinding her teeth together, and I had an uncontrollable, almost explosive erection.

"It's my turn," cried Radu, whose excrescence struggled to get out of his layers of fat. I didn't let him until all the soap and foam on that girl's body drained through the grating of the drainage, from behind which my poor manhood began to glance upward with a bulging eye.

We went to the basin with cool water, where our senses calmed down a little and went back to normal, and our barely unleashed testicles, like bowstrings with their arrows ready to shoot, rose coldly toward the places from which they had not long since come.

"Come on, tell us how it was with the circus-folks' daughter," they asked me with curiosity. "Did you fuck her or not? Come on, tell us." Each one filled his story up as much as he could, and the others knew that everything had to be taken with a grain of salt. From my silence they couldn't even get *that* much, and then I had to move my hand in a "so-and-so" gesture. They stared at me with a mixture of disappointment and satisfaction, finally happy that I hadn't gone past them.

Mircea, the oldest of the Podaru brothers—he was about 18—rarely came with us, and when he did we used him as a mentor. He was the only one who was sleeping with a woman, and a married one too, who used it out of necessity when her husband was gone.

"Fuck them now, boys, long as you don't get them pregnant. At least mine is married and she may as well have it, if it happens."

"And when can we get them pregnant?" I asked.

"When you start ejaculating."

"And when do you know that you've really ejaculated?" They all burst into laughter, like great experts in jerking off. My status in their eyes went back to what it had been before.

Tightrope Walk

Those moments were among the very few when I forgot Nora. It was clear to me that something weird, troubling, painful and especially abnormal was happening with my body, but also with my mind, which was stranger and stranger to me.

From one day to the next it seemed to me that my arms and legs were no longer totally mine, and I wondered at them the way trees wonder, perhaps, at how their branches grow in the spring. My eyes seemed to move farther out and I saw new things with them, which I have no idea where they were before that, and I especially saw myself, deformed as I was, as if I had gone out of myself like a sleepwalker on the roof. At night I dreamt that I was walking on a tightrope without any net underneath. I no longer fit in myself and I had nowhere to run. I vibrated; I was myself the diapason that was the tone of a universal trembling.

Someone unbidden was being born inside my shell. How can you not be afraid?

I was growing, I was getting taller, and my thoughts were spreading uncontrollably like a flood into a house where all the pipes are broken. Foggier and greedier, the whole world wanted to pass through me. A scary defilement, an invasion of ghosts, God's own ghost, whom I didn't understand anyway. And me, scared out of my wits, I wanted to do something to defend myself, but I didn't know what and anyway, I couldn't do anything.

When I got back from the common bath, squeaky clean but with a frown on my forehead big as a furrow, I went to sleep and slept three days in a row. I dreamed about Nora the whole time. In the dream she was well, in a protective aquarium in which only we two wallowed. I saw the outside world hazily and misshapenly through its walls. The ocean waited impatiently with all its sharks to swallow us up, whirlwinds, lots of whirlwinds, salty water, the filthy plankton of our already-programmed existence. We held our breath only at the thought of our spilling over, and I think that this is why I didn't want to wake up anymore. We loved anywhere, anyhow.

When I was awake, I spoke with no one about my passion for Nora or my new crisis. I would surely have lost my voice. I saw I-don't-know-what French-Italian film with the boys, and scrawny Nora was in all those beautiful women, large and wide, including Sophia

Loren. I could feel even her balmy shirt's smell. At the first love scene I simply drowned, as if I'd remained suddenly alone, at the bottom of the aquarium.

The beginning of a new school year was fast approaching. Another useless and stupid battle, part of a long and boring war called education, from which we'll come out defeated without fail, tortured, mutilated, if we won't know how to protect our poor nerves with lots of laziness and carelessness. The only thing that made us sharpen our pencils anymore was the fact that the school and its enormous yard started immediately next to the square's fence. Half of the gang studied there. In the fall, the gym would open too, which made the school hours somewhat more bearable.

It's proven that people grow more in their sleep, and I brought this to a test, because after two half-times of that narcoleptic sleep, I grew so big that my father's clothes no longer fit me.

Mom turned to the shirts and pants that were leftover from my uncles, her two brothers, who, alongside the fact that they were both doctors—hence people of wealth and more rows of clothes—were also very tall and handsome. I dreamt of becoming like them, but I couldn't decide which one I looked like more, and they, though brothers, were very different from each other.

My mind was in terrible modeling form: whenever I put on their jackets or pants, I went directly into their skin, through a mimetic process that said much about my unformed personality. If I put on the clothes left by Uncle Ion, so called "tetea" because he was older, I developed a slight nervous tic with my head. I started pendulating it to the front, as if I'd fallen into continuous approval, but doubtful of certain facts that I had to accept because I had no choice. I would also become slightly sullen and capricious, with exaggerated contemplative tendencies. In his clothes I didn't feel like doing much; the desire for action went away, but the imagination ran wild, so that I could travel anywhere with my mind. Precisely the vehicle that I feared most back then. Several times I grew horrified, because I went so far with it that there were only stars, planets and a universe around me, and it seemed that I no longer really existed, and that our worldly life is no more than a madman's delusion. I did, however, have a great desire to read. I made my peace more easily with words than with nothingness, though they too troubled me with their hidden meanings.

"If it were up to me, I wouldn't want to do anything, despite having a great zest for life," Uncle Ion would tell dad over a glass, without ever having heard of Zen philosophy. "I'd sit on a cloud and look at you guys, how you agitate yourselves over nothing. I'd read a good book here and there, chat with an intellectual angel and leave medicine." He was a dermatologist, and it seemed to him that skin diseases are too complicated and incurable, so he passed on to epidemiology and became the head of the Sanepid and did unannounced inspections of restaurants and cafeterias throughout the county.

I don't think he wanted to exile himself on that cloud alone, because he liked women. He moved to Ionică's house, into a room that lay right by the veranda, and once in a while he was visited by women and ladies that carried themselves conspiratorially, as if they were going to get vaccinated for smallpox. Through the wall that separated us, I would listen with an upside-down glass, eager to find out what was happening there. Ionică wasn't married either, and only a door separated our rooms. Even though my folks had put a closet next to it, you could still hear the groans and rhythmic creaking of an old bed that had been falling apart for three generations.

When I wore Uncle Luțu's clothes—my mother's much younger brother—I was energetic, full of grand plans and ready to mount an imaginary horse, very familiar with conquering windmills. He also had a tic. He seemed to loosen an equally imaginary tie that fastened itself again on his neck. When he told a story, he had a verbal tic, "Let it be," as if nothing had been but was anyway, to our puzzlement—those of us for which the world remained a worldly miracle deserving to be explored from the bottom up. He was an internist, and when his brother decided to go into the Sanepid, he decided to leave the country.

As different as they were, they got along well with each other, and mother, a fine observer of my disconsolate moods, gave me their mixed clothes, Tetea's jacket and Luțu's pants, to balance me out. Mom consulted them as doctors when my transformation started to seriously scare her. They both smiled and advised her to leave me alone.

Changing Times

I t's clear to me that something essential happened to me at that age. A biological earthquake that brought nothing down, but changed the whole order of things within me. It turned me inside-out so I could see myself from within, and then back around again so I could see all of it and live without cares again. The sweet and healthy carelessness without which I would have died on a daily basis.

Everything started when I could no longer stand the real change in an outside world which—I don't know why—I desperately wanted to stay the same forever. This sort of conservatism, inexplicable in a child, could only come from the depths of my cells, which had begun to multiply according to new laws that were far beyond my control. Every outside change hit me directly in my plexus, and I saw them all as another mutation that would lead to an inescapable checkmate.

One day, they started taking down all old, wooden telegraph poles in the neighborhood to replace them with solid, straight cement ones, which I didn't like at all. I couldn't shoot my arrow at them anymore, but this wasn't the problem. I simply liked the old wooden ones, sloping in all directions like crooked crosses. I imagined a crucified Christ on each of them. Just to clarify—I imagined Him, I didn't see Him—the wires that passed from one cross to another held in his multiplying hands. The electricity that Lenin himself had promised us came through them. I had a hunch that soon the day would come when, looking at the sky, we'd see its blue and clouds through a web of wires scattered everywhere like sky-piercing grills.

In the square, important people came who did some tests, glancing through devices on tripods. They measured our neighborhood like evil tailors who wanted to clothe our town in mocking clothes—our town, which, no longer a stately medieval knight, had turned into less than a beggar. They told us a whole neighborhood would be built right there in the square. I almost fainted at the thought that they'd chain us in concrete casemates with lots of pipes, wires, and faucets, and I was right to shake all over, because this is exactly what they wanted to do. Back then, there was only a single two-story "apartment complex" in the entire city, an ugly box that some approached with yearning, others with contempt. If you said you lived in the complex, people knew where you lived.

What upset me most was the disappearance of the steam locomotives that, to me, were sacred monsters that had to be protected by law. I had chained myself blindly to the serpentine image of the trains of yesteryear that crawled like tired dragons through the Transylvanian hills, with the puffing wagon up front and the almost-solid smoke left behind like a strolling inferno of fire and mist. This strange attachment tied me to Gil, who also loved the steaming locomotives—silently.

School started, and this inevitable event gave me an extra shock after every summer vacation. I was going into my last year and high-school admissions would follow—meaning serious rote-learning—a situation I couldn't see myself in given my morbid imagination. I was new there too but had the good luck of getting into the same class as Emil; we sat next to each other till the end of high school. Soon as he got up, the guy gave off an unbelievable vibe; he was a talkative, positive, loud sort that irritated many people. On the first day he picked up a fight with some older boys. According to the laws of the Hrube Gang, I had to jump to his rescue, and I came home with my clothes torn and a black eye. The next day, according to a well-devised plan, the two older boys got it bad from the Podaru brothers. Radu and Emil lay down when the other two got up, only to be knocked down to the ground on their heads. In short, the boys in the gang were all trustworthy; you felt yourself protected, belonged to a group that had solid ideas, a vision of life that lay outside the norm. Beyond this childish order, any other spontaneous, democratic method of organization was unthinkable. You would wind up in jail or in a madhouse, the only true refuges for adults. We'd long gone past the Pioneer and future Communists phase; those things couldn't fool us anymore. Might the desire to prolong our childhood have been, back then, an instinctive method of protection?

Radu came up with the idea of a 5-lei-per-month membership fee, one of the few ideas he got from the real, communist word of the adults. With the money we'd buy cigarettes, some sweet liquor that the girls liked too, and matches from which we got phosphorus for our loud pistols. His dad let us build a log cabin in a walnut tree, and we had our "headquarters" there that we climbed to on a ladder and where we could do whatever we wanted.

It was clear that the adults envied us for this passing freedom. Just a little and we'd be like them, closed off, with work, meetings, bosses, closed zippers on our mouths and ties around our necks—in a concrete cabin in an apartment complex.

In the evenings we'd gather in the square, and when the fruits began to grow ripe, we'd rush to the yards. The main victim was our music teacher, who threw me, Cretu and Emil out of the choir because our voices were changing and we were "ratting horribly." He stopped the entire choir and only had us sing, because he'd noticed that we were just moving our mouths in an almost-perfect playback. He had apples, grapes and nuts, and we stole them as soon as they ripened. He saw us one night, and a big scandal came out of it that wound up with our grades in "Behavior" coming down—a more important subject, for the future Communist, than math or history.

My folks didn't punish me too badly because they'd observed that for some time I'd had a more and more tormented look. Mom, who used to strike me daily with her palm or something in her hand—such that I didn't take her seriously anymore—no longer touched me with anything and asked worriedly:

"What's the matter with you? It's like you're not yourself anymore."

Around October, when the days had gotten shorter, I didn't even feel like going to the square anymore. I stayed home and stared blankly through the window without looking at anything in particular. On my good days I read. Nothing from school. The books I carried in my backpack every day seemed awful to me—to quote Emil, "a waste of time." I re-read *Les Miserables*, then Dumas, Tolstoy, history—no joke, it was a great world, even though during the revolutions they'd cut off their heads for nothing. After that I got into Greek myths. That mix of gods and people, which death alone kept apart, fascinated me from the start. The reading of books took me out of that changing world and gave me the illusion of changelessness.

For the first time I started being afraid of death, though nothing solid threatened me. A different death than the one that preys on us every day, which we don't care about because otherwise we'd go insane. At 14 it seemed that the future had disappeared. It had suddenly been swallowed up by a wicked and greedy God, a different God than the one my grandparents had me pray to every night. I was afraid that I'd disappeared imperceptibly into his belly, or that I'd melt like a bunch of ice left in the sun. It's so hard not to understand—but especially not to be able to go against things. Impotence doubtless has a worse taste than rotten fish.

That's when I decided to tell mom that dark thoughts coming from afar were on the prowl for me. I don't know what I said or how I said it, but I worried her pretty badly. She was quiet for a while, looking at me differently than she had used to, as if she wanted to say: "Let me think for a bit."

Instead of rebelling and distancing myself from my folks, which is what normally happens, I got closer to them, like a refuge found miraculously, high up in the brains of the mountains I'd strayed into. Dad didn't yell at me on a whim anymore, but he also didn't know what to do. He had always been a fighter, a man who didn't accept surprises easily, taking life's shocks as great injustices of fate. He'd growl, he'd rage, he'd fist-fight with the inevitable, but in the end he'd accept it. He was good to us. I only saw him drunk once, and then he became so exuberant and joyful that we almost hoped he'd drink more.

Mom accepted the offers of fate from the very beginning, like a price that always goes up, which is better to pay on the spot, without comment. But she liked to negotiate, and her wisdom was like the mysterious scale in the kitchen which she knew how to load just from sight, even though she adjusted it now in one direction, then in another, according to rules that she alone knew. Everyone who got to know her well valued her natural instinct for noticing the hidden nature of people and of seeds that are about to sprout. She didn't know what to do and how to help me. She decided to send me to my grandparents', at Bârla, because she knew that I had a special connection to old people.

When I got there, another hit below the belt. The whole village was in the midst of change. Half of the old, wooden peasants' houses, with porches, verandas, inclined gates (cracked but beautifully inlaid, covered with shingles or even straw) were taken down, and people were furiously erecting brick houses. Boxes, too. No one really worked the land which had passed into the state's ownership—meaning nobody's—but since they'd all been born with their sleeves rolled up, they had to do something. They would mix clay and water, mold the result into shapes, and the bricks were done. There was dust everywhere, since we come out of it and go back to it—after all, that's what the priest said in church to help them make their peace with fate. The bricks were burned on a smoldering fire in an ad-hoc crematorium; and look how easy it is after all to build a solid house. Caught in working the soil, they kept on wondering why they hadn't done that for hundreds or thousands of years. Grandpa said there's a good in every evil.

I was glad that my grandparents' old house was still standing, though leaning strongly to one side. I hadn't observed the great collection of bricks in the back of the yard, still hot.

Not even the carriages that swarmed through the village had their old wooden wheels, resoled with iron heated in fire by the village blacksmith, which made the pebbles on roads gnash their teeth. The peasants would steal the rubber wheels from tractors and other farming vehicles, which were no longer theirs; they'd jump proudly and elastically over the jacks, their voices no longer trembling from the shaking while they sur-rounded and whipped their emaciated and headstrong horses. To cool down a bit, they'd unload on the poor animals which they'd torture in all sorts of ways, hitting them as if they were guilty for what had happened to them for centuries.

Grandma would scold grandpa whenever he was upset at fate and the communists in particular—she'd complain now about the oxen, now about the dog, even the poor chickens before their end in a pot. Sometimes she even picked an argument over the bees, which he took care of like his own eyes. On the other hand, they loved their animals, and it hurt them when they had to butcher them.

On Sunday I went with them to church. The peasants still dressed in colorful popular costumes, the same ones from when the world began. They didn't have it in mind to change the church, at least, though they did deserve a bigger one. Those same Christs cut out of painted zinc boards, nailed at the village entrances and in front of the church, had rusted and lost their color, moving and rattling whenever the wind blew.

"If you look carefully," grandma said, "his wounds and blood have stayed just as red, with all the wind, rain and all this weather. It's really a miracle." Since she never needed eyeglasses, miracles were clearer for her.

"When we were Greek-Catholic we have some pretty, freshly made Jesuses," added grandpa, who you could never tell whether he was joking or serious.

"Quiet, someone can hear us." That's how grandma would end many public conversations, and it wasn't clear whether she was talking about the divine ear or the hidden eardrums of those with a hammer and sickle that could be continued directly with the stirrup and anvil in the inner ear of you-never-knew-whom.

They avoided the priest too. They had all been Greek-Catholics until around '48, when Catholicism was forbidden in Transylvania, and the church became Orthodox overnight. The Communists didn't fear Christ and his wounds so much as the Pope in Rome, who, human as he was, could meddle in their affairs. I knew this from grandpa, who sometimes let himself speak freely around me.

The service had something enlightening, old, if not primitive, ready to satisfy my strange need for stability. I liked it, but its length exasperated me; during that time, I'd rather stand up like at the Last Judgment, or kneel and supplicate until my growing joints would start to pop. The smell of incense made me feel guilty that I'd started to smoke so early, but it drowned me pleasantly, like a gas coming from the heavens.

Everyone went home penitently, grateful for the priest's enlightening words; they ate, fed their animals (which they'd eat later) and got ready for the round dance. Only I and some old ladies, frightened of the death that was inching in on them for real, remained in the church. Grandma spoke with the priest about doing a service for me that would "untie me." Untie me from what, I had no idea. I didn't feel tied to anything. On the contrary, I felt like I was spreading out. The priest didn't ask me anything, just like that, to see what was wrong with me, and he did his duty as if I were at the dentist's. He put a stole over my head and began to pray for my wandering soul, which wouldn't find its river-bed. A whirling, muddy river, possessed by who knows whom, into which too much water had spilled, and so on and so forth. Lord have mercy, Lord have mercy! I automatically felt like saying, in the midst of all the solemnity: The priest catches the fish in the sea. Amen. Grandma, who assisted piously, payed. And so we left.

On the way back I felt somewhat better, and this only because I wanted to get to the round dance to see them dance. The girls would redden their cheeks with God knows what paints, which made them look like dolls about to burst with good health. On their chests they put necklaces with heavy silver coins from the days of the Empress Maria Theresa. The men wore rattling bells on their feet over well-shined boots, which they'd worn since at least the days of Franz Joseph, and in their midsections, they wore beautifully ornate, wide leather belts where their families' entire wealth could fit, plus a penknife. The bench near the fountain where the "Americans" used to sit, those weird old folks who had worked in the old days in boiler factories in Cleveland, remained empty. They'd all died without getting to see their lands bought back with dollars. The gypsies would tune their instruments, oiling their bows with resin, and start the music after dampening their mustaches in beer.

The round dance surely has something magical about it, like all things that give rise to dizziness. People smell one another, pinch one another, go round and round till they go into a delirium that rises slowly and doesn't just come from alcohol. The women and girls don't even drink, but they seem more fired up than the men who plump up around them like frenzied roosters. The old folks stand on the side and watch, and the older they get, the harder you'll be able to guess what's in their heads.

Only Romanians were there. The Saxons and Hungarians had their own "round dance." People only mixed when they worked, and it seemed like that was enough. They spoke at the bar or as neighbors, over fences, on holidays. Each prayed, danced and died in his own language. Each knew what was bad or well with another, but in the country they were all peasants. Meaning they loved their land, their soil which had been taken away from them and which they clung to. They all had WC in their yards, on the same soil, and they never went on vacation. Who ever saw a peasant on vacation? "Maybe these people fired us," grandpa would say, and we didn't understand. The Romanians and Hungarians, with all the squabbles between them, sometimes married one another, after which the couples would go to the city. The Saxons and Jews didn't really get to mix with them; they left early to Germany and Israel.

The father of a good friend of mine, a Saxon from Sighișoara, was a prisoner of war of the Russians for six years. They used to be neighbors with Obert, another Saxon from Sighițoara, the one who invented the racket and who, much luckier, had been taken by the Americans. Mr. Markl ruined his lungs in a Siberian mine and payed, like so many Saxons from Transylvania, just for being German. He succeeded in running away, and after several months during which he only traveled at night, he arrived at a village where he was hidden for a long time in the house of some Romanians. They dressed him in trousers, those long, heavy and hard wool pants, and put sandals, a shirt, a girdle and hat on him. They tried to teach him to walk with a swaying motion, to sharpen his sickle quickly, to cross himself from the right to the left, to hammer nails crookedly, to spit like a Romanian. Hard, very hard. How could a German learn all these things easily, one born into a family of Lutheran pastors who had worshipped in the great cathedral in Sighisoara for several generations? His ancestors had been neighbors of Count Dracula's, had built some of those Medieval houses with meter-thick walls, where today there are wineries and must cellars.

His father, the priest, was addressed by his mother with "Mr.", and the Romanians tried to educate Herr Markl to say "well" instead of "aber", how to whistle in the alleyway in his misery, because times had changed. Most things didn't stick to him, though he tried. When he went to the round dance where he was to see his darling returned from Russia, the mother of my friend, a Saxon masked as a Romanian, they gave themselves up after the first spin. You can't dance what you're not. They escaped because the times had changed again, just a little, just enough so they wouldn't wind up in Russia again. They changed their names from Markl to Marcheli, which was something more Latin even though it didn't sound Romanian. They emigrated later to Germany.

Round-Dances, Songs, Charms

When, at the round dance in Bârla, I paid attention to their rhymed shouts, through which they communicated loudly and publicly to the rhythm of the music, ironizing themselves sprightly or making proposals. They were better at rhyming than our Romanian teacher, who tried unconvincingly to get across to us that folklore might be a real treasure. I didn't hear any shout where "soil" might rhyme with "oil" because then the entire folklore would have gone crazy. Sometimes they got angry and drunk, and fought or took out their knives. That's when the policeman would come.

On the second day, I told them I didn't care about school anymore and that I wanted to stay in the country for a while. I would pick out authentic folklore from house to house, village to village, before this national treasure would disappear along with the steam locomotives and the old wooden houses. I asked my grandma to get some old trousers ready for me, and some sandals and hard linen shirts. I had it in mind to note down the words she sang all day long, cooking or cleaning the house. I remember grandma singing all the time, praying or running after the chickens and chicks in the yard, trying to catch a fatter one for the lunch meal. That's how she died, years later, on a day when she found out we'd all be coming over in the evening for dinner. She got excited over catching a chicken and had a fatal stroke.

In those changing times, they got pretty scared of the crazy things coming out of my mouth, and great-grandma took the reins. I called her "old mother", and she was around 90, but no one knew her exact age because her birth certificate got lost in the days of the Austro-Hungarians. She and some old women in the village knew how to do exorcisms in smoldering coals and to rid people with an evil eye of spells and charms. Christian women that through invisible channels kept alive the link to the old world of fairies, spirits, familiar to the Dacians, Gepids, Cumans, Celts, Slavs and others who haunt harum-scarum through Romanian veins.

The old mother took her role very seriously. She spoke rarely, because she was a woman that seemed to have said everything she had to say in this world a long time ago, and in any case it was hard to understand anything she said because she didn't have a single tooth in her mouth left. More than anything, she would hiss the words that she chewed between her gums like seeds. That day she spoke clearly, bluntly, as if all her teeth had grown back. The coal exorcism involves taking some hot pieces of recently burned coal straight out of a burning furnace. The peasants' hands are so calloused that they could carry the fire itself in them. The old mother was very dry, and I was afraid that she'd catch on fire and burn in front of us like a splint. She threw the piece of hot coal into a pot with water. While the coal sizzled, crackled and gave out steam and smoke, my great grandmother had whomever I had to be untied from.

First on the list was always the woman. "If a woman gave him the evil eye, may she writhe around, her eyes pop, her gallbladder grows, till he's uncharmed." I had only seen Nora, who could be "the woman," about to explode undeservedly, and I left the room furiously. I didn't want to be untied from her or from our bond and marriage. I heard on the porch how the unclean one, the man, the gypsies and others, whether willingly or through carelessness, could have ruined the peace of my thoughts. Nine coals had to be thrown, I remember this number well, as if nine alone could have been the number of the evils that loomed over me.

In the end I had to drink from the water where the coals fell. It had a horrible taste of lye. They were looking at my head hoping to see some change, as if my thoughts would have become visible like grandpa's bees when they come out of their hive in the spring. Stooping, great-grandma also extinguished some supplementary coals and mumbled something weird with her eyes closed, and grandma prayed to the icon of the Virgin, but I held on to my own. What's more, after I threw the water with the coals, I saw a beautifully painted ceramic on the bottom of the pot, with the year it was made inscribed on it: 1832. The cat that followed the whole procedure, frightened, happy that it wasn't mentioned among the possible evils, was eating from a slightly cracked dish. I set it aside, and among the bits of stew and bones I could read 1802. I thought I'd go nuts.

I gave them a long discourse that scared them for good. I called them unaware, irresponsible, vandals, because they had no idea what things were hidden in their own household. Look how today no one cares anymore about the past and its footprints, which are trampled on, given to cats to lick and so on. Starting tomorrow, perhaps, we'd start some archeological digs right there, in the yard. I saved the pots; they still exist today. Then I made a succinct inventory of the house, and I asked my grandmother to leave me her necklace with silver coins after her death. And if I would no longer be, to donate it to the museum in Bistriţa.

At the Psychiatrist

That's when my parents got scared for good. They decided to take me to Dr. Nica, the psychiatrist, the one in our county who decided who was insane and who was normal. The truth is that I also wanted to chat with an expert of minds, to know once and for all what was the matter with me.

Once home, I started yapping. I wanted to communicate desperately with the adults, to test them, to test myself, to see how they'd react to all my obsessions. It was clear to me that such bizarre ideas had no place in the normal skull of a kid. What was serious is that I was suffering terribly, and the undefined fear kept on growing. At night, when we went to sleep, I held long discourses, because I felt instinctively that talking helps. The words that came out of my mouth made me feel alive, even though they chained me like heavy links to a brittle world that, with or without my will, would change. Plus, I was also trying myself. What was true was that their increasingly alarmed faces weren't too soothing. They sat up on their feet with their legs crossed Turkish style between the two beds; I slept with dad in one and my sister with mom in the other. I kept on talking nonsense about by favorite subjects: the disappearance of folklore, forests and steam locomotives, the dangers through which our maidan was going because of the ill regard of the local politicians, and especially how I didn't want anything in this world to change. I tried to explain to them, in my words at the time, that my perspective had purely and simply died and that I couldn't see myself at 20 or 30. I couldn't even see myself at the end of the upcoming winter. To convince them, I would put my hand over my eyes as if I were staring far away into an imaginary horizon and tell them:

"You look at this, too. Nothing can be seen in front of me."

Sometimes Uncle Ion would come too, also in pajamas. He'd wobble his head in his nervous tic, like a dermatologist who doesn't feel right when the conversation turns to mental problems. Instead, he'd bring me a white loaf, because he ate only loaves, which for us had the value of cake. He was on the ration stamp; my folks didn't have relations, so we had only black bread in the house.

"I'll talk to Dr. Nica to see him."

At the end I would recite to them a popular verse, usually wise, but very defeatist, which jolted them out of their sleepiness and made them stare at the ceiling until morning. My sister seemed the most worried. Later, she confessed to me that she was scared for me, but also for herself, with whom I was so closely tied to genetically. Puberty had begun visibly in her too, but it treaded beautifully and gently, through the front door. She would have liked to speak more with me, but she was afraid.

What was for sure was that I couldn't leave childhood, like an egg in which a worm, grown too big, remains a moribund prisoner. Everyone started treating me with a kind of fear, not to mention pity. I no longer thought about Nora truly and passionately, as if she too had gone into the fog of the past. Mom provoked me to speak about her, about our walk with the elephant, on whose spine she suspected that I'd learned what love is. Any subject was to be preferred to my silences and idiocies. I couldn't concentrate at school anymore. I'd look out the window at the cathedral's spire, following the hands of the clock, which marched forward peacefully and in equal steps toward a future that I excluded myself from.

One morning, we dressed nicely and went to Dr. Nica, the psychiatrist. A tall man, middle-aged, who covered his baldness from left to right with long, greasy strands of hair whose proper maintenance took up half his time. I was prepared to tell him everything. What hurt from the very beginning was that he didn't look me in the eyes at all. It's OK, I told myself, a doctor who treats crazy people from morning till night is probably fed up, even scared to look into their tormented eyes. I had come of my own goodwill to give myself over, and he didn't even encourage me with a glance. On the other hand, I looked straight at him, absorbing his reactions, grimaces, beads of sweat and the lines on his forehead, between which my diagnostic could have come at any moment. The first thing he said to me was:

"Aha, so you're only 14. I thought you wanted to avoid the army. And what's the problem, young man, eh, tell me?" He looked at me for a fraction of a second, and it seemed to me that he had a pretty warm and humane look. Too bad he didn't use it more often.

"Doctor, to be honest I'm afraid I'll go nuts. Everyone thinks something's wrong with me, and I think they're right. But what's worst is that I don't feel good anymore in my own skin. If you have patience, I'll tell you some of my thoughts, so you can see for yourself."

The doctor didn't seem to have too much patience or time, so I didn't have an opportunity to go into one of my long tirades. He pretended to write on a white sheet of paper, but I saw across the desk that while he was talking to me, he was drawing or sketching something.

"Tell me if you hear alien voices that speak to you."

"I hear only my own voice, which doesn't seem to be mine anymore since it got thicker."

"And what does it tell you."

"Only idiocies, doctor, I can't tell you."

"Come on, tell me. Don't be embarrassed."

I got quiet, and he no longer insisted.

"Sometimes I hear a huge diapason that rings in a third ear, one that sometimes, from somewhere high, gives us our tone, as if it wanted to bring into unison a choir that sings falsely with every voice. At school they kicked me out of the choir. I ask myself whether I'm the only one who hears it, maybe…"

"I understood this thing with the diapason." He seemed to note something. "Tell me if you happen to have hallucinations.?" I looked at him surprised. "Meaning to see, to hear things that don't exist in reality."

"Doctor, not long ago it so happened that I rode an elephant at night. I was with a girl with whom I'd done fooled around, you understand what I'm saying, and that night I came across some gypsies that—you won't believe me—married us according to their custom. We were perched on an elephant and then, to answer your question, it seemed to me that I could see weird shadows, I felt other smells, I heard this music. They gave us a pipe to smoke from… I don't know what was in it… I keep on thinking about that girl, the elephant, the gypsies, about…"

"Enough, enough. Have you ever thought about death, somehow, in any way?" I gazed for a long time at him again, but he continued to play with the pencil. "For example, being in a church tower and wanting to jump off?"

"Only if I had wings, sir, otherwise how? But since you're talking about cathedrals, I'm obsessed by the old clock's hands, the big cracks in the church's walls. I'm horrified that one day it'll collapse on us, and the clock, how can I put it, will swallow time up and blow it over the town like a poison that's been gathering for centuries. If I knew how to draw, I think I could…"

"Enough, enough. Even if you don't know how to draw, here's a white sheet of paper. I want you to draw a tree while I'm in the restroom."

"Why a tree, doctor?"

He didn't answer my question, and he left. I noticed that the entire hallway and office were full of drawings and pictures showing trees. Trees blown by the wind in all directions, with leaves, without leaves, some with their roots growing upside down, some uprooted, their branches in clouds; oaks, junipers, everything you could ask for. I quickly drew a straight and white tree that resembled our birch in the yard, whose every nook and cranny I was familiar with. Then I got up and looked at the sheet he left on the chair. He had also drawn a chair. Stuffy, big, many-branched, which went up or went down, depending on how you saw things, like a family tree. When he came back, I sat down quickly, as if I'd just been discovered copying in school, and I handed him my tree. He didn't look at it too long and he put it in my file, which I hoped would remain thin and which I would have loved to read, to see what he wrote.

"All right, young man, that's enough for now. I'll talk to your parents."

That was it and not a word more. I went out confused by the mental hospital's hallway, where my folks were waiting anxiously, as if they were expecting a grave verdict from a tribunal. They went into Dr. Nica's office, which they left with the same puzzlement and fear in their eyes.

"What did he tell you?"

"He said that we'll see," said mom. I got angry without suspecting that my rebellion was a sign of mental health. I mean, to see what? Am I or am I not OK in the head? Does the tree of my mind have its branches, its roots the way it's supposed to, or does it grow wildly in the blowing wind?

Things remained tortuous with Dr. Nica and, if he's still alive, I might still be on his list of possible paranoiacs, schizophrenics, manic-depressives, and who knows what other disorders described in the only psychiatry book that I saw in his office.

Calcium and Bromide

This event made my mom meet with Mrs. Rusu right that evening—a medical assistant who lived several houses uphill. A decent woman, who always asked us how we were whenever she met us. That's how she came across my story. Mom invited her over to our home, and after they had their coffee with sour cherry jam, they started to notice me.

"Don't be afraid, Adrian dear. I have three grown boys and I thought I'd go insane with each one of them when they reached your age. One of them is a lawyer and two are studying architecture. It came to them one by one and all of them got well after I gave them intravenous calcium. I only went to Dr. Nica with the first. You're not crazy, boy, and if you are, then the whole city is crazy and there's nothing you can do about it. Look how much you've grown in one summer; you're taller than everyone by a head, and your bones have eaten all your calcium. I think there's a calcium problem in this entire region. Maybe in the whole country. The mind doesn't function well without calcium. Starting tomorrow I'll come every evening and I'll treat you like my own boys. It won't hurt you, and you'll see how slowly all of these stupid things will leave your head."

Mrs. Rusu suddenly instilled more faith into me than all the psychiatrists in the world could have done. It's important to know that it's happened to others and they got well, as with any illness. They sent me to the maidan, so they could talk more.

Pişta had just tried to gather people for one of his wild ideas. This guy didn't worry at all about his mental health, even though it was clear that he wasn't all there. No one thought to take him to a psychiatrist. Pişta had declared a life-or-death war on all the cats in the neighborhood. He would bait and catch them and put them into a bag that he hanged on a tree. I never assisted in his cruelties, but I knew what he was up to from the boys. The cats meowed and struggled and, before the execution, he would consult formally with his twin brothers, whom he horrified using them as witnesses and jurors. Both of them ate chalk and plaster from the neighborhood houses' walls, which they picked with their fingers. Maybe they too lacked calcium, but their instinct of self-preservation was better than mine. What's more, the paints and materials were full of lead.

"Well, boys, how will we get this done?" Usually, he used a mace onto which he'd hammered some nails, and he struck the sack until the cat stopped meowing and blood flowed from the sack. He forced the young kids to hit the sack, too. He would tell them the cats wanted to eat their carrier pigeons, the only beings he seemed to care about.

When I started growing house rabbits in the yard, I called on Pişta once. Some relatives of ours had come to dine with us. My folks hadn't been able to catch anything to eat, and then mom decided we'd have one of my rabbits. In the beginning I was against it, but then I felt useful and asked Pişta to come, who butchered him happily. Because it was a sacrifice on the altar of our empty bellies, I clenched my teeth and even decided to make an effort and help with the whole process. Before Christmas, when grandpa butchered the pig in Bârla, I would run to the rear of the orchard until they put the knife in his throat and he stopped grunting.

Pişta did it professionally with a special knife that he brought from home. I still remember the sharp blade going over his throat, the cutting wing of death, the blood spurting from its carotids and the perfect silence of the rabbit, who seemed an accomplice to everything that happened. He nailed his fur to the restroom door in the yard. Later, Pişta started working at the city's slaughterhouse, where he became the boss.

Mrs. Rusu would come in the evening with her syringe kit and sterilized needles. She would suck calcium out of three vials with a very small syringe, fasten the tourniquet on my arm, look for a needle whose end wasn't too bent and she'd tell me to turn my head and look at the picture on the wall. Our only picture, which I knew by heart down to the smallest leaf. A road on the outskirts of a forest leading nowehre, a house with a fence in front of it, near the fence a child painted disproportionally small in relation with the rest of the landscape, several small sheep and a big dog or wolf (not sure). Intravenous calcium heats you up terribly; you see green stars and feel it in the form of a peculiar taste on the tongue. If it's not done slowly, you can faint, or your heart can stop beating. Push the syringe's piston a little faster and farewell growing, becoming, depressions, worries, girls, women, marriages, children, divorces, emigrations. Life.

It wasn't calcium bromide. It was gluconic calcium, I remember it exactly. Calcium bromide had a peculiar reputation in Romania. It was said that it tames our manhood, our cravings and desires in general. It could be put into our tea, coffee or food. We had to be careful about this everywhere, especially at campv, cantonments, gatherings. In the army they even made mashed beans with bromide. Toward the end of communism I think they put it even in bread, water, air and televisions. *Can't you see that it's not going up?* grown men would say. I think it was an exaggeration, like that about the gypsies stealing children. How could there be so much bromide?

How well Mrs. Rusu knew to make intravenous calcium! She had blue eyes, beautiful and kind, like my grandma from Bârla, who she resembled, though she didn't sing. She would push the piston of the syringe slowly, and I had to tell her when I started to feel hot and not see clearly anymore. She told me in detail about her sons' breakdowns, each of whom had his own transitory madness.

The lawyer had been much worse than me, and this calmed me. He would wake up at night and wander randomly through the maidan where he saw places that didn't exist in reality. He had begun to believe in kinds of ghosts and unseen parallel worlds, inaccessible to our senses. After he had read a book about India, he wanted to convert to Hinduism because he was convinced that reincarnation was real. He desperately wanted to find out what other lives he had had before, as if he'd existed before being born. Thank God such nonsense didn't go through my head! It made your hairs stand on end. He believed that the body that grows from week to week and which functions, of course, only on the basis of calcium, is merely a transitory vehicle. At 15 he had run away from home and was taken by the police in front of the Indian consulate in Bucharest, where he tried to enter at any price. He wanted to convert to Hinduism and Buddhism and had read all of Mircea Eliade's books. Pure madness, if you ask me. Just thinking about the poor boy made me feel better. Anyhow, I would have liked to meet him.

After about a week, I started to feel how that magic calcium began to deposit itself and harden over my fluid thoughts, like a calcio-vecchio splattered over a moving wall. My uncles would bring me vitamins and fish oil, which mom filled me with. What was true was that my thoughts hadn't changed suddenly, but they didn't torment me anymore. I still carry some with me, like a ballast that I can't escape from. I didn't care as much about steam locomotives, forests and folklore, and I started to go out in the maidan with the gang. Once in a while, I felt that I could hear the tone of that celestial diapason vibrating at a distance that I couldn't tolerate. I would stop foolishly in the middle of my tiny life, like a stranger at a forbidden pedestrian crossing, and I would ask myself foolishly: "Who the hell am I, with these hands, this nose, these thoughts crowded together into my Adam's apple?" In time, I started to ask myself this question more and more rarely, and not because I ever found out the answer.

One night I dreamed that I was making out with Nora and we were doing those beautiful, painful, shameful things—I don't know what to call them—in the back of the yard, only that in the dream everything was stronger. Feelings that passed through the jammed amplifier of my senses. In the morning, my pajama was seriously stained, and mom washed it without a word, glad that I was no longer holding discussions at night and that I was finally sleeping.

Around then I also received a letter from Nora. I opened it feverishly, but it was very difficult to

understand her writing. A scribbling, difficult to deci-
pher, as if she'd written with her feet. People raised in
the circus! She called me "my love" and continued with
the promise that tortured me that "next year we'll end
what we started... wait for me." This made me ignore
the delay and illiterate writing. In the meantime, I'd
found out through traditional methods that I was "ejaculating." So I could have left her pregnant, according to
Podaru's theories and the natural laws of nature, which
starting at a certain age become unforgiving.

Boys all masturbate at this age, but they all do it
quietly, thinking that they're the only guilty ones in
the world. At school, naturally, this wasn't talked about
during classes. What girls did I had no idea, but after I
grew you couldn't find one who would prowl through
your pants. You couldn't talk at all about sex with parents because they would pretend not to hear or smack
you on the spot. It was clearly a conspiracy on every
level, one meant to keep us in the darkness for as long
as possible.

In those days there was a single radio channel,
something like Radio Yerevan, abstract-cipher-hu-
moristic, which dealt with sexology. The questions and
answers were so ambiguous that you had no idea what
they meant. It was like they spoke in code. They'd ask
questions like "if we do it too often, what can happen?"
I asked Podaru about what those shows were about,
and he convinced me that it was about jerking off and
nothing else. I picked apart the problem with the boys,

ambiguously of course, and Pişta said that he knew for sure that excess could seriously affect your spine, which would start to flow out until it ended you. His folks told him, and other adults confirmed it: doctors, psychologists, medical assistants, specialists. He said he wouldn't risk anything for the time being. Killing cats satisfied him enough. I grew horrified.

According to this theory, perhaps subversively put forth by the authorities themselves, our nervous systems are diabolically linked to our penises, which would pump everything most precious to us into noth-ingness if our hands helped them. From the spine to our thinking brain. Hunchbacks were most suspect, so I had to walk as straight as possible.

Anyway, I told myself, it was healthier for four of us to stay in one room, plus the grandma from Năsaud who slept in the winter on a sofa that blocked the door, thank God. What could you do but stare at everyone as they snored carelessly, as if they breathed the essence of bromide? I finally understood what Mrs. Rusu meant when she pumped calcium into my vein:

"I felt like tying their hands, nothing else!"

When I would go to the WC in the yard, I'd put my hands on my nape, as if summoned from behind.

I only received one more letter from Nora, even more illegible than the first. "It's hard for me to write… I miss you…"—that's all I understood. It was clear that with that kind of writing she hadn't gone to school. Where could my illiterate acrobat have been? The more illumined my mind and feelings became, the more I started to miss her. Her sweaty feline odor, her movements, her ribs which came out of her skin like the claps of a sensual accordion that played by itself when we kissed. Surely she would have grown too, had grown larger if she ate well and if the trapeze jumpers weren't torturing her anymore. I had no doubt that her emaciated hips had grown a bit and that her tiny and hard breasts had enlarged. There had already been clear signs.

It was harder for me to fill the emptiness in my soul those days, though children tend to do this without trying. Forgetfulness came faster only because time passed slower. A summer vacation was like a year. Later, I would come to understand time like a kind of whip. I speak of the time that belongs to us, that unknown that was assigned to us at our birth. A big whip with a ball at the end, which tortures without touching us. It goes in circles and tightens around the cane, ready to snap. At first in big circles, large, slow, then you don't even notice that it's gone over your head. As it shortens it moves faster, more frenetically, like our years, until the rope runs out. Crack!

That summer was the longest in my life. It was a veritable jump through time, in which the circling of the whip seemed to have stopped. And this scared me more than anything else.

At School

Emil was the sort of boy who wasn't at all in the mood to lose his time with the banalities of puberty, to which he seemed as immune as to a smallpox he had had in another life. He had unconsciously made the decision to pass directly into manhood, without acne on his face, without hidden thoughts, without useless breakdowns. He was red-cheeked, his glance was straight and his boldness touched the limits of insolence. He grew slowly, normally, without getting entangled in his own movements. He was so different from me that he couldn't not attract me. People made from a different element, those I thought I couldn't imitate, always fascinated me. I didn't think back then that this lack of mimesis could have been one of my advantages. At that age I wanted to change, to be different, and it was no wonder that I didn't feel good in my own skin.

In the seats in front of me sat Eva and Rodica, two girls that bloomed before our eyes. I had learned their tresses, their braids, the stains on their uniforms, the down on their napes and their growing forms. On some quizzes I would copy, hiding sheets under their skirts, which were mandatory down to the knees. I knew the teachers wouldn't dare search there. Rodica had such long and hard legs! I had a close collaboration with her, cramming all five great writers that I knew would be on the Romanian quiz under her skirt. From the knees up, in the order of likelihood, with Caragiale on top, crammed under her panties. He was on the quiz. She sat with her elbows on the table and pretended to concentrate with her eyes closed, and I would search under her skirt for the sheet. My fingers dampened as I sought after the essence of Caragiale's works, which had become hard to read and reeked heavily of woman. I was best in literature, but I needed another four years, fool that I was, to take it further with Rodica. I had a short but powerful love affair with her, right when I finished high school and was walking around with our farewell serenades.

Emil got with Eva in the first trimester of high school. When I say got together, I don't just mean that they held hands. After my experiences with Nora, I thought I was pretty advanced for our age. But at the end of high school Emil told me how Eva's mother caught them during recess butt-naked, making love as love is really supposed to be made. Her mother was a judge at the tribunal and with all her prestige she was barely able to unglue them, that's how intertwined they were. They were 15. They reached a compromise with the judge, like at tribunals—a compromise they alone know. After high school they remained together, then they married, had two children and are still where I left them even today.

With Emil I had my first attempts at escaping reality. He had a healthy, creative imagination, which back then outdid mine, poor muddy magma that still floated in fog. My restless spirit, suffocated between cells, hormones and anguish, didn't anticipate the great migrations. At that age Emil was the one who seemed to be the adventures, the potential refugee. How differently we evolve in the end, how unforeseen! Worse than butterflies, who are merely crawling worms before they fly.

In order to make the class hours more bearable, we determined to imagine that the places at our desks were places in front of a Volkswagen. This was only one of the exercises. That's how we started one day to live in an imaginary world, because a mini Volkswagen belonged to the realm of the fantastical. We'd seen one in the city, brought by a German who'd left and, alongside the six Moskvici taxis that had replaced the old wild thyme that surrounded the train station, it seemed like the tip of a provoking, spreading phalange of putrid capitalism that had begun to bait us.

We tried to travel through the country with our minds, or even abroad. Only that here, imagination no longer helped, because none of us had been further than Năsăud, a city that you could easily imagine without having ever gone there. In the beginning, we took turns at the wheel, and then we decided that one day we'd live in England with the wheel on the right, another somewhere in Italy, with the wheel on the left. Whenever I left or came to the desk, I would mime the opening and closing of the creaking door, the contact key, the arrangement of the rearview mirrors and everything going through our heads. Everything was a continual pantomime. The one who had a real clownish vocation was Emil, and he never lost it. If we had to go to the board, we'd park the car first, hit our heads against its low roof, open the doors (which creaked) and get off with difficulty, numb from so much driving through Europe.

The class would laugh. Sometimes we were thrown out. After a while, they left us alone with all our virtual worlds. It's one thing to have an imagination and to know how to use it, even in idiotic situations. People respect you even if you seem insane. Whenever we mounted the horse too hard, Gubesh, the biology teacher, gave us a choice between digging holes in the school's botanical park and shaving our heads. We would choose the holes, which had to be a meter by a meter, "for some imaginary trees, boys". After he measured the holes, he would make us put the soil back. Smartasses that we were, we "planted" a thick palm tree here, a virtual banana tree there, exotic trees that we marked with real plates.

Attics

I like attics, with all they hide under their thick layer of dust, pigeon shit, mice, bats and spiders who can jump in front of you when you least expect it. All homeowners cram their past into their attics. It's the best place for it. You rarely climb up there. The past might as well rest in crates and corners. There, photographs become yellow most easily, and forgotten letters can keep on talking to each other as long as they please. The dead beneath the soil, their traces in attics—that's all that remains.

The attic of the house in Bistrița was a veritable graveyard of memories, and if you went through them, you would find unexpected things. Old letters and postcards with beautiful, calligraphic writing, pictures of long-gone people who look you in the eyes and know how to keep their heads proud. I stayed a couple of days in that attic where I found out that Ionică's grandma,

our host, had cheated on her husband with a cloth mer-
chant who wrote her rhymed poems on pieces of silk
cut out from reels in stores. Between two beams, which
closed at a weird angle, I found a sword, and when I
stretched my hand far I came across something metallic that wound up being a German pistol with a full
barrel. I was slightly scared, and I thought that it was
not good to rummage like that through other people's
pasts. You never know what you can come across. I
refrained with difficulty from pulling the trigger while I
aimed through the glassless window of the attic toward
all the people who replaced the polls in the neighborhood, the steam locomotives, the wagon wheels. It was
hard for me to pull the sword from its sheath; it had
rusted a little. I wiped it with my shirt and decided to
put it back behind the beams. I gave the pistol to my
father, who grew horribly pale. I don't know what he
did with it, because it disappeared with the gun, and
I suspect that it's rusting somewhere in the waters of
Bistriţa, beneath the bubbly gaze of fish.

In the evenings, even though it had gotten cold, and
the days were shortening like clothes in water, we were
outside in the maidan till late at night. The future had
begun to open up more and more parentheses in front
of me. We'd gather in the cabin in Radu's tree, where we
played cards or made plans. George, after lots of plead-
ing and lying flatteries, helped us clandestinely pull
two electric wires that ended in a bulb. One evening,

to finish it off, he invited me and my sister to his attic, where we suddenly entered an unguessed-at world.

George's attic looked rather like the lab of a converted alchemist, who combined science and magic without realizing it. Both at our communist level, where everything mixed with everything else until it became unrecognizable. No trace of the past there. It smelled rather of the future, even though our future was like air and water, odorless, colorless and tasteless.

It was immaculately clean, a pharmacy-attic, because George couldn't stand messiness. Every wire that left some device, coil or battery knew exactly where to go and what it had to do. You only had to protect your head from them. There were notebooks full of formulas and hard problems everywhere, completely solved, and books and lots of physics and math magazines in English and German. Einstein's picture on a wall, but not the one with the tongue sticking out. On the other side were Marx and Lenin, who gazed dispraisingly at Einstein, after all nothing but the representative of capitalism, a loafer as relative as his theory.

I tried to ask him what he was experimenting with in the attic, but he didn't answer me, as if he were forming some secret there. In a corner he had a strange radio he'd made from scraps, a box where he listened to Europa Libera like any self-respecting adult who thought he wasn't watched. That's where I heard the Beatles for the first time; they were singing *Michelle, ma belle*, and I fell in love with them on the spot.

When Gil saw George's attic, he completely forgot about my sister and proposed a profitable business venture. They were wonderfully compatible when it came to this. They were formidable guys, and I—that calcium not having completely hardened yet over my mind—well, I couldn't quite decide which of them I wanted to be more like. They were so different from each other, and both of them from me. After long discussions, they developed the first clandestine shirt printer in the area, if not in the entirety of Transylvania. We also wanted shirts with famous heads on them, famous singers, weird dragons or just a sign with "no war" or "Give peace a chance", which didn't bother anyone ideologically. Since I got along well with them, I came to possess a blue shirt with Che Guevara's head on it, which I wore proudly for about three or four years, convinced that he was Jimmy Hendrix.

One spring day, well before school ended, George suddenly disappeared. Everyone shrugged their shoulders when you asked them about him, including his parents, who seemed to hide something. No one heard anything about him until the fall, when he appeared in the maidan with unusually long hair, dressed in an original blue-jean costume, and a shirt where the four Beatles were passing proudly over "Abbey Road" between his pecs. We all envied him to death. He seemed like a weird foreigner, the way he chewed his gum with his hands in his pockets, from which he took out some blades for us. It was with him that I chewed those first concrete samples of the West. I was like an infant, who perceives the world by putting it in its mouth, and that gum was our first direct contact with the West that we all sampled with our decalcified teeth. Only George's face, that of a trueborn Năsăudean, and his heavy Transylvanian accent kept him in the frame of our collective canvas. He told us he went to Germany to see some relatives, with an attitude that he had just visited his grandparents in Năsăud.

That fall, after the start of school, two black Mercedes, whose front seats I would not have dared move in my desk and Emil's, stopped in front of his house. The whole neighborhood went to their windows to see what was happening. After a few hours George came with a large trunk in his hand, surrounded by two fat and sweaty individuals, and he was taken away. It would be years till I'd see him again.

George had a subscription to an international German physics magazine, which published very difficult problems to solve. Those who solved all of them had been invited to an international physics congress for young people, in Munich. So that's why he wasn't playing with us in the maidan! Having some connections at the passport office, he was allowed to go to Munich the way people went back then—quietly, on their tiptoes, no noise made. There, at a large university, after more than a month of competitions, he won first place in the world, succeeding in finishing the most interesting project tied to the energy consumption of a building with over twenty-five stories. For us, something dizzying. Back then, not a single building in Romania had passed the fifteenth floor, and we hadn't even seen that one.

The Bavarian newspapers were filled with his name. He'd made several thousand marks, and when he was about to return through Czechoslovakia, the Russians invaded it with their tanks and parachutists. Caught in Prague in those days, he began to admire the Russians for their demonstration of power and remained convinced for a long time that they were the ones who would rule the world. When the people in Bucharest found out about his exploits, they sent the two Mercedes after him. In a short while, George became a true national treasure.

On the Ice

In the winter after that calcium cure, I began to feel that my mind had grown enough for me to get rid of my morbid fear and my absurd obsessions. I never got rid of fear completely, as if it were my own shadow that grows and thins according to the sun, the planets under whose sign I was born, and especially the people gravitating around me.

The Bistriţa River had frozen around December and stayed so for a long time. The entire city was encased in a thick layer of snow and ice. I went on skates more often than on my own feet. A new kind of skates had come out, which could be tightened with a key on the soles of the boots, like metallic carps. They'd stay stiffly there all day, and because of that, the soles would loosen and break easily, and no one would repair a pair of boots twice in a winter. When I walked without them, snow and water would get into my boots, and in the evening, when I took them off, I'd have a bunch of ice between my toes.

My folks sent me daily to the bakery to get our bread rations. Waiting in line, all we children were there with our skates tight on us, and we irritated the saleswoman with their metallic thumping. After cutting out the day on the ration book, she'd throw me some pitch-black bread. You knew how time flew and what day it was just by looking at the monthly bread ration-book. I don't know where Uncle Ion got those white, thick loaves. It was worth becoming a doctor for that alone. Today I miss the taste of that bread—I mean the black one. Besides having the taste of my childhood, I've found out in the meantime just how healthy it is.

On an early March Sunday, the weather had warmed unexpectedly, and our whole gang went to the river to skate again before the thaw. On the sidewalks the first spots of cement were appearing, and above us, under the eaves, big, deadly icicles were aiming for us—

which, had they struck, would have gone straight through us. Every year, the tiny avalanches that started atop the old three-story houses buried some old, deaf woman in cement. In the river we had our own place at Codrisor, the same where we bathed in the summer, and a deep whirlpool where the remnants of a bridge that the Germans blew up when retreating stood on each side.

After we passed from hand to hand an unfiltered cigarette, we went to the frozen river, which may very well have coursed in any direction to a stranger who didn't know the place. We skated through dozens of bends and windings and were to regroup near the old waterfall. I still wasn't in the best shape; I still had the slow and unsure motions of a convalescent, so I remained with George, who skated prudently and carefully, as if someone had made him draw straight lines with his skates in a notebook of ice. Only Radu the Fat was behind us. I could hear the creaking and crackling of the ice that felt the coming of spring better than we did. A couple of times I'd see cracks in its gloss, which spread like spider-webs behind us. I arrived before the rest, who had already finished another cigarette. Evening was coming; the purplish sun was casting a strange and oblique light, and the chimneys in the city between the hills were puffing away straight lines of smoke that rose stiffly, unusually high.

On our return we had to skate fast. The first to get to the broken bridge would receive 5 lei from our common funds. They all sprung to the chase—the Podaru brothers, Emil, Gil, Tanase, even Rodica Deac, who always competed with us, even in arm-wrestling. With our national hero on the 5 lei banknote in mind, I kept up with them through the first bends in the river. Then my knees failed me and I kept pace with George, who was waltzing slowly and methodically.

Radu was behind us and was trying hard to catch up to us. I could hear his wheezing and heaving on my nape. I could hear the cracking of breaking ice behind us. We both turned around. Everything that followed has lingered in my mind like the re-winding of a horror film. The ice had broken underneath him like glass. We were in the middle of a river that begun to melt, and Radu was almost totally submerged by water that bubbled to the surface like a hidden dragon. We got close to him, close enough to see his bruised face and his hands clinging to the edge of the ice. I wanted to help him, but I stopped, frightened of the ice crackling all around us.

"Don't get close!" I heard George saying behind me, a strange mix of shouting and whispering. Radu suddenly disappeared beneath the ice like a ghost, and we stood motionless, sure that everything would collapse around us. When Radu got under us, I saw his frightened face. He stopped for a moment and stared at us through the thin and clear layer of ice, as through the window of an aquarium of death. He was hitting it with his fist and trying to tell us something through the bubbles that were still coming out of his mouth. I almost wanted to shout: "What are you saying, Radu?" but he disappeared underneath the ice that had unbelievably spared us. The rest also saw him passing, his face upturned. He got to the bridge before us, and when he got past it I don't think he could feel anything anymore. They found him two weeks later at the confluence with the Someş, when the river had thawed.

George, whom I met after a couple of nights of narcoleptic, tortured sleep, told me that maybe we were "chosen" to escape. I think this idea of "chosenness" took charge of his thoughts for a while. Maybe Radu had also been chosen. Neither then nor since have I thought that I'd been a "chosen" one. The simpler notions of luck and fatality sufficed for me in those days.

Death itself didn't scare me too much. What horrified me was Radu's so-sudden disappearance, the way he passed at once from one world into another just like that, through a simple fall, without having the time to get his thoughts in order and say something in the end. I suddenly wanted to go to church with my grandparents, for someone to guarantee me that "Indeed is He risen!" That Radu would someday re-emerge from beneath the ice and that we all carry the seed of eternity in us. In those days I was ready to become the most fanatical Christian if someone could settle the problem of the resurrection for me. At such an age, it's hard for death to scare you, even if you've seen it with your own eyes. In the end it was too distant a concept, too abstract—something only others had to deal with.

How I needed a tender letter from Nora in those days of mourning! Anything, illegibly as she wrote. I could imagine the rest. The whole neighborhood was sad and mourned. Everyone stared at us coldly. They felt we were guilty—especially me, the "chosen one." I don't think guilt has anything to do with age; mine grew like a tooth cavity. George was touched too, but he said we couldn't have done anything except go under the ice with him. He went back for a time to his lab in the attic, where he began planting the seeds of his future, without knowing it.

For a while we all stayed home, ruminating on our sadness. Pushed forward by the same guilt, I tried to flip through the schoolbooks, work that gave me headaches, nausea and deep sadness.

Businessmen
and Adventurers

I didn't see Gil until the summer, when everything had bloomed and we'd started going to the woods nearby. I felt that he was avoiding us. Sometimes I glimpsed him walking alone in a green, almost military shirt, which made it hard to see him in the thickets on the outskirts of the woods. The woods were his experimental attic, where he was as secretive as George.

He was the strangest kid I'd ever played with. I kept in touch with him for a long time, until long after we'd stopped growing, had begun shaving and moving from one place to another like firm men. He stayed the same—almost linear. I never saw the trace of a crisis in him, not during puberty, not after. Gil seemed to pass through childhood as if it were a miserable period, a duty from which he tried to escape with all his might.

He didn't know how to play. For him this was nothing but a big waste of time. He always smiled, but he never laughed, and I think that maybe he had instinctively intuited the depth of the desert this world was sinking in.

Whenever we met, he'd come up with an idea that was the beginning of some new business plan. I don't know why he chose me specifically for a partner. To him I wasn't a Bohemian, as I was to George. Gil's imagination was boundless. What can be more beautiful than making grandiose plans that you're not even bound to start! Gil's tragedy was that he didn't like to leave things unfinished. Sometimes his ideas were so complicated and strange that I thought we were only playing games.

Our first cooperation was the train business. The railroad was right around the block, and we both loved it like it was our second home. We'd fallen in love with the steaming locomotives, as if they were good, child-loving dinosaurs. For us they were the puffing symbols of true freedom. Back then we wanted to become train-mechanics or even stokers. They always travelled. In the station they'd stop the fast trains with tourists coming from the sea, or from Budapest or Vienna. The trains were fed water and coals, and people came merrily to the widows. Gil would start chatting with them at once,

"Mulberries, apples, pears, pumpkin seeds and sunflowers!"

Our bags were filled with everything. We'd rip the pages from our notebooks and make cones with them. For the most part I was on the side, munching on the seeds ashamedly.

"You're a fool! Go walk by the wagons with your bag open and at least smile. If you're ashamed to work and make money, stay home and play with dolls!"

Gil had a lot of money. He re-invested it in other business and even made a workshop in his basement. Sometimes he secretly lent money to his mother. She was an educated woman, surrounded by books and musical instruments. She always told us to learn, and when we would grow older to get away from this small town. Advice that we would quietly follow.

Right around then we also started growing doves called letter carriers. They were trained birds, with pedigrees, marked on their legs with special rings. We would take them to the hills or bridges around, where we let them go. They always found the way home, as if they were teleported. One day, we were selling our agricultural products as usual under the windows of the Vienna express. A girl around our age was sitting by one of the windows. It suddenly seemed to me that she resembled Nora, and my heart began an unexpected gallop, like a whipped horse. Perhaps my former lover is also abroad with the circus. I hadn't thought about something like that yet. Perhaps that's why she wasn't writing me. Who would want to write someone left off on the edge of the world, because Gil said that where we lived, it was the edge of the world. The girl wasn't Nora, but the galloping in my heart went on for a while. Gil started chatting with her and found out that she was going to Vienna with her parents.

"We envy you, young lady! We're not so lucky. We're not going on vacation anywhere. I want to ask you something special…" He took a shoebox out of his suitcase, with the lid full of holes.

"In this box there's a carrier pigeon who always comes back home. But he's never gone too far. Tomorrow, when you arrive in Vienna, please let him out through a window."

The experiment interested me too. The second day I was at his home waiting for the bird. Gil was working on a Pinocchio in his workshop. He'd already done several, and they looked like wooden phantoms hanging on the walls.

"There's a big fair on St. Mary's," he said. "And then I'll sell them all. If you help me paint them, I'll give you three lei apiece. You waste all your time playing foolishly."

Toward the evening I heard a murmuring in the yard, and I knew that the bird had returned. But I saw no joy on Gil's face.

"This is a true champion!" I told him admiringly.

"He would have been a champion had he stayed in Vienna! But he has no brains, poor thing! You can imagine that yesterday this idiot was perched on the tower of some cathedral in Vienna with the whole city at its feet, but he decided to come back here, to us, who stay here and never go anywhere."

The experiment failed here. Then he sold all the marionettes and doves. I took my part of the profit, and for a while I avoided him. I'd had enough of business.

But our last strike was unforgettable. The same grocery store where they sold vegetables and fruit collected old iron, and so we both started a cleaning project of everything in the place that was iron and could rust. I think we only missed the rails of the railroad and several heavy sewer caps. The country needed steel, and it paid well. We forgave nothing metallic that came our way, including a kitchen furnace, still hot, and several screwdrivers left by the railroad workers for the following day. The people at the grocery store were already seeing us as suspects and asking us when we would bring a steam locomotive. The idiots had no idea how much we cherished them.

With the last transport, on the other hand, we brought a bomb from WWII. Undetonated, of course. I came across it playing in the enormous school cellar, somewhere in a hidden corner where the teachers kept their potatoes and carrots for the winter. I knew from the start what it was. I had seen enough war movies, and it seemed to be one of those bombs that fell from planes. God only knows how it got there, and I swear that it never went through my head that it could still explode after so many years of disuse. The manager of the grocery store was a German who had been in the war, and when he saw both of us carrying it inside and throwing it on the scale, he threw himself on his belly under the counter.

"No one move, you wretches!" he cried. We looked with satisfaction at the scale's needles, which moved gratefully. What followed was unbelievable. The police came, then the army, and they evacuated the whole street. They arrested and interrogated us for hours. Our parents too. The bomb was then detonated in a field by military experts. The whole town resounded with its bang and the smacking I received from my folks in exchange.

Then the great scandal followed. It was fall and school had started when Gil disappeared without a trace. His mom, the police, and professors came to me to ask me if I knew anything. I saw him very little after the story with the bomb. Gil had become even more isolated, even more quiet. He was brought back after a week by the police. He had been arrested by the border patrol at the Danube's bank, where he was taking off his clothes to go into the cold October water. He had a large sum of money on him. Yugoslavia was on the other side of the river, then the paradise of the West, after which were Austria and all those countries I'd found out about in geography class. He got off easy then. They took him to a doctor, and they blamed puberty with its torments. His courage shocked me. He later confessed to me that he'd been planning that for two years. He wanted to travel the world and do business in a grand style. His enterprising spirit, unusual at such an age and for the place where we lived, was seen as a weird and incurable malformation.

Blood Brothers

We had built a large fire in the woods, one of those that in a drought-filled area would have thrown nature into the flame and scorched thousands of acres of woods. For the third time, I'd seen a German film with Indians with all the gang—*Winetow*—where the white man, as he diligently conquered America, found time between massacres to get close to the Indians with whom he'd establish close bonds of friendship. Some, like Old Shaterland, a German emigrant from Montana, gets close to Winetow, a tribal leader, and they become brothers of the Cross or, as they say, blood brothers, according to the laws of the unchristen natives. For this they had to mix their blood after making a cut in their arms. We had decided to do the same thing. Not out of solidarity with the poor Indians, which I felt instinctively close to, but rather because of a premonition. We felt that soon our gang would burst and that no matter how long we'd try to keep our childhood going, we wouldn't be able to stretch it out much longer. It would end like those cigarettes we smoked ferociously and that melted by themselves even though you didn't take drags from them. The better they are, the faster they will burn. We knew we'd pass imperceptibly into a world that was muddy and full of adults' lies.

Around that time more and more people had started to appear in the maidan, determined to measure, parcel things out, and nail poles, people who acted as if no one was there, as if we were just a tribe of Indians who had to be chased out and put into a reservation. The great invasion of cities was getting prepared. That's why I think we retreated to the forest nearby where we decided, in our desperation, to become blood brothers. Not like in the German movies about Native Americans, where people become brothers in pairs, but the whole gang at once, mixing our blood according to rules we made up.

We weren't all there. The idea scared some for good, and others probably didn't want it. Gil shrugged indifferently and didn't come with us. Such unnatural bonds didn't interest him, and he wasn't to be blamed when you took into account what he was hatching. A man who wants to jump the border doesn't care to tie his life and soul to some rooted plants like ourselves, who couldn't dream further than the skulls that shielded their marginalized minds. It was as if you had mixed blood with chlorophyll. George said he couldn't do something so unchristian, especially since he'd had hepatitis and he wasn't in the mood to catch another one from us. They didn't know I'd been to Dr. Nica and that my blood was pretty decalcified. We all hoped that that moment of ritual brotherhood would hold us together in a magical way, forever, like a beautiful contagious illness.

I think there existed in us something primitive, like in all men, something tribal, atavistic, because we excluded the girls. Rodica Deac also wanted to become a sworn brother to us, but this time we gave her a cold look, like a poor cat that tried to mix with tigers. How can you become a blood brother to a girl! We dreamed of entirely different conjunctions with them.

Pişta was sharpening a large knife on a rock. A special penknife belonging to Radu. I don't know whether the Indians or Radu's death, which we didn't discuss but never forgot, stirred us most. He was sharpening the knife methodically like a butcher, gazing at our faces, where fear and indecisiveness grew like the livid stains on a freshly severed head. He tested the knife's blade with his fingertip, and when he felt that it was just right, he planted it in a log in the middle of our circle.

"Who's first?"

We stared at one another, calculating our ages in our heads, thinking that the oldest should be bravest. Costel Podaru took the knife first and passed the blade softly over his wrist. Right where desperate people who kill themselves in bathrooms cut themselves. Several drops of blood came out of Costel's hand, like red and round beads of sweat. He handed me the knife. I closed my eyes and pressed the blade over my wrist until I felt it touch the nerves that spread through my skin. I started to bleed as well, the same red blood color as the geraniums on my grandma's veranda.

They all did it in silence, last of all Pişta, who was the only one to hesitate a little. We were all pale and moved, and not because we were letting some blood. We joined our cut hands one by one, greasing them with our mixed blood, now brothered. At last I took the shirt that Radu wore during the summer from my bag. We took turned wiping our bleeding arms with it. We had asked his mom for it, whom we didn't tell about what we were planning on doing. The poor woman didn't hate us; sometimes she even called us over and gave us jam and a piece of summer salami, for Radu's soul. In the end, just as we'd planned, I dug a hole and buried the shirt.

What's strange is that later on, as our lives started speeding up, I stayed in touch with George and Gil, with whom I hadn't mixed my blood, but with whom I entangled some thoughts down the road.

Summer Vacation with the Girls

The schoolyear was closing in on summer vacation like a sinking ship full of holes. Lessons were the last thing on my mind. During class time, perhaps due to the silence, the discipline forced on us and my freely wandering thoughts, my desire to go into a woman came back. Stronger than ever. I would have gone in not only with the thing that was rising in my underwear dozens of times per day, during all subjects, including math, but with my whole being, which struggled either with the spirit against matter or vice versa. My matter became more and more erectile, always ready to spew forth its frustrations and unfulfilled desires, which I mastered with difficulty, like an unskilled mercenary of life.

I took the girls in the front row one by one and imagined that we would do all sorts of things. There were also one or two younger teachers that inspired me. Nora and what I had started with her in the haystack was of course the basis from which my imagination took off. Had I guessed then in how many ways one can penetrate and come out of a woman, as from a beautiful and damp trap, I might have gone mad for good. It was hard for me to go with my imagination beyond what I knew, but sometimes, especially during biology and Romanian class, I got to doing all sorts of new and brave things in my thoughts, the way I thought Nora would have expected of me.

I had no patience left. I had to do it before Nora's return, so I could calm down and initiate myself into the great mystery of the great unknown's penetration. I wanted to make her happy. Because it was clear to me that there had to be something magical in this joining together. Something more than the physical act per se, easy to imagine if you imagined that crack, softer and more slippery than your own hand.

I was tall, and my voice had thickened. I joined the town's sports team, and I could say that I was pretty agreeable to girls up to a certain point. What I lacked was boldness, and since their breasts and thighs had started growing so much their initiative had also died. We all changed. No grown girl would have thought about going through my pants.

I would have loved to take a hike to Şieu, to see Laura again, the policeman's daughter, who had been so greedy with me not long before.

On a Saturday I took the train to my grandparents' and from there, on a bike, I only stopped in front of the school where I had lived and learned. I climbed the hill and looked at the village and the people passing rarely in the alley, and from the perspective of Bistrița, it suddenly seemed tiny and dead. The Wolf family had gone to Germany and their vineyard had grown wild, and weeds invaded their yard. I saw Laura, who had come out to the yard to feed the chickens. I almost didn't recognize her. Her curves were noticeable, like temptations hurriedly covered. I got up on my feet, put my hand over my mouth and called to her. I don't know exactly whether I said her name or just uttered a kind of howl like that of a moose in the woods. She turned her head and I waved at her. She gazed at me over the fence, unsure whether she recognized me. Then she opened up shyly and gave me her hand.

"You've grown so big," she said. "It's like you're someone else." She was someone else too. We sat on the steps of the house like two strangers, and we were quiet for a long time, thinking about the closet full of uniforms, naphthalene and foggy memories. I felt a kind of fear.

"Do you remember us two?" I asked stupidly. She nodded her head without looing me in the eye. I said nothing more, and she didn't give the impression that she was expecting anything.

She was scared too. We stood on the stairs surrounded by a perverse silence. Quiet and a little cowardly to boot, prey to the June heat and the hormones that swarmed under our skin, entire anthills of desires, legless millipedes crawling through us aimlessly, without a plan, just like that, to torment our lives. I tried, without being able to control myself, to smell her naked nape and her hair, but she pulled away. This was all I could do.

Around us, as if deliberately, flies were coupling like crazy. They flew two by two, clenched, so that they couldn't separate even in midflight. They would settle on us, on the grass, wherever they got a chance to, without caring about anything. Their self-preservation instinct had disappeared; there was a veritable sexual delirium in the air, a massacre, and the swallows preyed on them, two at once. They would settle on my arm and breed indifferently, passionately, between my hairs. I threw them with the tip of my finger into her lap, and they saw to their business there too. Laura finally smiled at me, but this was all I got out of her.

I gazed at her large and completely new breasts, and I thought that everything started from them, but I didn't really get how. I would have dragged her upstairs on the stairs to the uniform closet, but I understood that she wouldn't loosen up easily. What the hell had happened to her? It seemed to me that the year before, this girl had lost her memory or maybe pretended to be crazy. Where was her erstwhile initiative, when she would provoke me shamelessly and prowl through my underwear hungrily?

Things had changed radically. What an idiocy, God, what filth of nature this idea of female virginity, what a meaningless perversity that membrane of theirs put there, at the entrance to paradise, just to ruin all our joy. I imagined it as something elastic, which could swell up like a balloon, and into which I could blow hard and then poke it with a needle, just to see how it pops.

Then I decided that only Hilda could save me. Everyone knew she did it with the boys, even that her first man had been one of their teachers in the German department, who had almost lost his mind and job because of her. It was well known that German girls were more libertine. But how could I get to her colossal breasts? To her millions of freckles, which covered her large and milky body, islands of pleasure whose inventory I would gladly have kept, like a desperate and ignorant Robinson. Her red and very rich hair scared me as much as her reputation, but I got most scared when she revealed to me plainly that she was a romantic first and foremost.

I didn't expect that! She made it clear to me that if I wasn't able to feed this defect of hers, I had no business anywhere near her. All the guys who boasted that they'd been between her legs either played an instrument or were in the school's literary circle. Hilda herself sang at celebrations, recited German poetry with difficult rhymes and had even published in their paper, which ended with the word "Zeitung". None of the boys spent too much time with her, and this experience was marvelously convenient to me. I only wanted a small sexual stage with her before Nora's return, a small initiation and consolidation of my masculine pride and daring.

What's true is that Hilda attracted me, a solid creature, a Nibelung and a Romantic at the same time. As often as I spoke to her, she looked me straight in the eye with an interest that I couldn't explain to myself, much as I made things up in my search for arguments. Emil encouraged me, saying that Hilda was exactly the morsel I needed.

I convinced my folks that what was missing very much from our home was an accordion. This was because I'd decided to start playing an instrument as soon as possible, seriously and with both hands. I impressed them with my desire to play *The Blue Danube*, and since my other obsessions were still alive in their minds, they relented, loaned some money and just like that, picture me with an accordion hanging against my chest, under the birch tree in the backyard.

At no point before or after that did they answer a request of mine so swiftly, no questions asked, no negotiating or conditions set. Later they confessed to me that they both loved this instrument and the idea of seeing me pull on the accordion's bellows on a stage overwhelmed them. The music teacher, a nice and youngish neighbor, volunteered to give me lessons. It was hard not to be moved by such a strong desire in a child who was willing to leave play and other pleasures aside for the love of music.

As soon as it came, it also passed. It was hard as hell to get all the claps that had to be pressed differently than how I'd thought, so that the melody in your head would agree with the sounds that came out of the instrument, which scared all the birds in the maidan. Nana saved me, a true sister, who accepted to take my place until my musical ear formed a bit. She took lessons for four years and came to delight us with *The Blue Danube* on Christmas or whenever we had boring relatives over. She abandoned it slowly as well, and the accordion has lain for decades in a corner of its box that no one has opened since then—out of fear.

I didn't give up, and I wanted to get into the school's band, as a drummer, but I gave up because I wasn't good enough, and Hilda grimaced when she heard.

I had only one solution left, which I could no longer postpone. I started writing poems. I, who wasn't even able to remember an entire short poem by Coșbuc. I wasn't even sure whether Hilda could taste something romantic in Romanian, because she wrote only in German, and when she recited during celebrations she put so much pathos and life into her words that she scared us. I was glad I didn't understand everything she said. At the end of the recital, she recited a poem about the party in Romanian, more quietly. I think she only did that so they'd give them a passport sooner.

When I told her I'd been writing poems secretly for a long time, she asked me to show her one. Even if it was in Romanian, it didn't matter; she had mastered my mother tongue well and said she liked it. I got to work that night. I started to sweat immediately from emotions and effort, since creation squeezes the life out of you. I didn't know why everything had to be rhymed. I couldn't decide which poet to imitate, so I leafed through some books to see where I could plagiarize most efficiently. With Eminescu, too famous, she might catch me; he was translated into German too. Coşbuc, Goga, no way, these guys were all about the homeland and she wanted to emigrate to Germany. Minulescu, Bacovia, possibly, lots of rain, like in our place, love and great, universal sadness. In the end, I got disgusted with myself and went to sleep.

I don't know whether I dozed off or not, but I suddenly started to see rhymes, clear, precise and solid, agreeing with one another like perfectly aligned soldiers or telegraph poles that come one after another from the perspective of a moving train, just as you'd expect them. Increasingly rare rhymes mixed with transparent images, feelings like in dreams, hard to cast into words.

Around midnight I got up and sneaked into the kitchen, where I spat out my first poem. Around five stanzas, pretty original, which have been lost, but with which I conquered Hilda. I only remember that the last verses were "with red hair and freckles", but I don't know what they rhymed with. That same evening we kissed in the park. She had thick and damp lips and an odor of foreign deodorant that puzzled my senses.

I continued to write rhyming poems in the kitchen. The girls in class were asking me to improvise some in their memoir books. They even published me in the school paper. I wrote easily, but mom started thinking again and asked me how I feel, her mind on the calcium injections. I cheated too. Hilda thought that all those poems were written only with her in mind. I thought more about Nora, who—let's not forget—remained my first wife.

I had lost my patience, so I tried more passionate poems to get between Hilda's legs as fast as possible. I had no doubt: based on how she kissed, how she breathed and how she closed her eyes, she must have been a great expert. These were clear signs, what more do you need! She even played to me on the guitar when she heated up. The dilemma was: where would we do it? In the end Emil saved me, who gave me the keys to the attic of an uncle of his who was gone to Bucharest for some time.

Hilda immediately accepted, though I wouldn't have gotten upset if she had delayed me a bit. We ran from school, and in a few minutes we were in a room with lots of furniture and pictures with people I didn't know and who stared bizarrely at us. I smoked a ritualistic cigarette, which she took a small drag from that made her cough hard. We kissed until her cracked lips began to bleed, but while she held a handkerchief over her mouth, she let me caress her breasts and unclothe her down to her waist, without resisting. Finally, a true woman. My heart swelled, as did everything in me that could have swelled.

"You know, poet, that this is about all we can do!" She disconcerted me suddenly and calmed me down at the same time. I was gallantly quiet, but I continued to play with her so long as she let me. I thought it was just a game to warm up. When I went for the attack, chaotically and clumsily, she got out of her trance as if I'd just smacked her.

"Stop!" She got up with me and she covered her statuesque body. "I like you, but I can't sleep with you." She read the amazement that appeared on my face, an expression probably never immortalized on any of the Greek statues of pubescent boys, and she left me to burn for a while.

"Come, tell me frankly, poet—you all think I'm a little whore, isn't that so?" She looked me straight in the eye, like the no-nonsense girl she was. "If I told you I've never been to bed with anyone, you wouldn't believe me. Come on, tell me!" I was contrarily silent, not knowing what to think anymore. Could there be so many liars on this earth? She then got naked. It was like the revelation of a real statue, only that I, the only spectator of that strange exhibit, no longer understood anything. I was dumbfounded and didn't know what to do.

"I trust you. I want us to make everything clear from the beginning. If you don't believe me, I'll let you look. You can put your finger there, but nothing more."

I didn't do any of this, I believed her word and I never again doubted her virginity. I was quiet, and she spoke.

"If you promise me not to go in there, whatever might happen, I'll let you stay next to me." I nodded like a bell without a tongue. This idea of "whatever might happen" sounded very good, it was an extra step into the unknown. I took my clothes off and sat next to her, or over her, I don't remember. Anyhow, I kept my word like an ass until she went to Germany, where she absolutely wanted to go as a virgin. Several times, all it would have taken was a little extra, a centimeter or two to spoil her honor for eternity.

During the time that we were friends, although I didn't say a word, her reputation in the town recovered, a change that didn't seem to give her any satisfaction.

It was fated for it not to work out and for me to remain partially a virgin until Nora's return. I don't know why this lack of progress seemed so embarrassing to me. I had this specific idea in my head that I, as a man, had to be initiated in the act of intercourse. It was like a duty, and this was because I had never forgotten that I was a married man. I thought many times that that entire procession with the gypsies who bound us together on the elephant's neck was only a fragment of my imagination.

I went into summer vacation resigned, almost pacified, convinced that I'd done everything I could have toward my initiation. If I could have suspected then how long this process of creation would take, I would have shuddered.

The Moon and the Gypsies

There was a month left until the circus' return. It came yearly with the precision of a traditional holiday, meaning sooner or later, but it would come. The first stalls of the fair and creaky horse carousel had already appeared in the square.

In order to get away from the summer heat, we would go to the waterfall, which was right outside the town and which produced electricity before the war. Everything was abandoned, and in the summer the town's bohemian and her children bathed behind a dam that was useless now. We bathed under a foaming waterfall which we used instead of the public bathroom, then we wallowed in the canal. Once in a while, someone would drown.

Around us it was full of bushes where you'd step on condoms thrown randomly, and if you looked deeper into the woods you could see bodies clinging to each other on hot days. That's how I came across a neighbor by mistake, a quiet woman married to a locomotive mechanic, who had a naked man between her wide-open legs who pushed himself into her with a frenzy that's hard to describe. I almost stepped on them. I was alone, only she saw me and put her fingers against her mouth to tell me to be quiet or to suppress her moans. I stopped; I was quiet and looked for a moment at how they were thrusting into each other.

She was staring straight at me with a contorted face. I had never seen two people entangled like that, and the sight shocked me as if I had just discovered the truth: that sex between men and women does indeed exist and is as disgusting and grand as between animals. I left and stepped carefully so as not to crack a dry piece of wood. I had heard that the same thing that happens to dogs can happen to people: that when they're scared, they can't get one out of the other, and then they walk on the streets like that, together.

Adults were nuts, no doubt, and look at how we couldn't wait to be like them. The next day I met with that woman at the bread queue. She came to me as if I were holding the line for her. She caressed my head and smiled like a perverse aunt that, meeting me randomly on the street, fills me over with makeup and compliments about my masculine transformation.

"You've grown so big! You know how to shut up, baby, don't you? I'll repay you for this, don't worry. Come to my house Thursday, I'll be alone."

I didn't go to her house that Thursday, not the next one either, but I kept my mouth shut. I couldn't see myself between that woman's legs, some lying pliers that ate up men as soon as her husband left. That's how I lost my last chance, like a huge idiot, doubtless a real chance from which I might have come out a man, though not a whole one. One that would have mercilessly duped one of the last steam-locomotive mechanics.

To make money, we hired our whole gang to pick strawberries, but the bad pay and a diarrhea that we all got kept us from going to the field. Money was paper as important to us as to our parents who, poorly paid, barely resisted getting additional wages in one place or another. Every night, my parents would note in a notebook how much they'd spent, how much they had left, how much they had to ask Uncle Ion for loans, how much they owed, what had to be absolutely bought and what not, when the boots full of holes would have to be covered. We didn't even dare to ask them for something. Too much money for books and cigarettes, mom would complain in the end, and I think her thyroid got sick from those calculations. A gland in the throat, exactly where she'd show us when she said: "It's gotten all the way here." She'd become irritable, got angry from nothing, her eyelids trembled, and it was hard to get on her good side.

I found work by myself at a deposit where I fixed broken crates from grocery stores. The packages in those days were more important than what they had inside—which was generally missing—and which made people break the crates angrily.

Every day a mountain of croaking crates that I had to fix even though they'd never be filled with anything waited for me. There, I only learned how to hammer nails straight, one after another, hour after hour, without hitting my fingers, my thoughts always elsewhere. The guy I worked with, a former theology student who'd been expelled, said it was as easy to give a sermon, saying the same thing over and over again. You hammer the fate straight into the soft souls of the parishioners, who pay you for that.

I hammered nails from morning till evening. After a while it calmed you, it emptied you, like knitting does for women. In order not to fall asleep, the theologian recited all the psalms that he could remember, with a voice that trembled with the rhythm of the hammer and with an intonation that wasn't Christian at all. When we went out during our breaks, he told me only filthy things. He never told me why they threw him out.

"It would have been good if I became a priest. I'd have been good, don't you think? Look, I think you'd be good for that, only you're too quiet. Do you have some voice?"

I had no voice, and I didn't know what I wanted to become. The priesthood had been erased permanently from my list. High school admissions were coming, but the tiny person inside me had decided that he only wanted to think about things after the circus left. Hitting nails, I quickly understood that I wouldn't like to do that for the rest of my life at all, and nothing similar either. I had to look elsewhere. My folks were more and more worried for my future, which they felt I was busting stupidly. They hadn't started to bother me, because they were afraid to mess up the tiny wheels in my head again. They'd just been greased, and they still creaked.

One day, the boss at the deposit came and told us he'd go home sooner because he wanted to see the American moon landing on TV. It was 1969. The Americans were conquering the moon, and we were fixing putrid, empty boxes. I threw my hammer, and after that day I never went back to the deposit. The theologian smiled perversely.

"I'd like to know what the bishop and God think about this Moon landing thing."

I went home to Gil, who had recently bought a Russian TV. The whole gang was there waiting to see the miracle. Gil was on the roof trying to get the antenna to work, as if pointing at the moon would have made everything clearer. I saw the man stepping on the moon, bouncing like a ball, leaving his footprints on the lunar dust, as if he were in his own home. The American astronaut suddenly seemed like one of those people who stuck cement polls in our square, and a familiar feeling, which I had thought I'd got rid of, struck me in my plexus.

At first, we were all quiet, then the adults started talking in doubt about the truth of what they'd seen.

They doubted their shadows, but mostly they doubted the words. Especially those that came from radios and TVs, which sounded empty, like rolling conserve cans. They'd been waiting for the Americans to get them out of the mess, and instead of coming to save us they'd preferred to walk on the moon.

The second day, I went to my grandparents. Things there were still like in the Middle Ages, and even though they dug the earth and went on building new houses, you felt safer there. Half the village didn't believe in the moon landing, just as they hadn't believed Gagarin's flight, and this was yet another reason why the world would end soon. The invasion of Czechoslovakia the previous year was yet another reason why our days were numbered. In the countryside, people had a strange doomsday instinct. Whenever something happened in the outside world and the shockwave reached them, they were convinced there wasn't much time left. Some resigned themselves calmly and didn't even go work the land anymore. It would have been a redemption after all, fate's revenge. I think it was convenient for them too, though I don't really think that they thought the apocalypse that knocked on the world's door would reach them. They were so far from everything.

Grandpa used to say that the world had simply changed or, more precisely, that "the world wasn't the world anymore."

The following day, he took me to a hill where they still cared for the remnants of a vineyard that the communists had forgotten to confiscate. He wasn't sure whether the vineyard was his or not, but he went on working and making wine from it. All day long I tied the offshoots that otherwise would have invaded everything around. At night I slept in the vine cabin. I had a cigarette in my pocket, and I waited until he started snoring to sneak outside. I went up the hill, where I realized that I had no matches. I tried to get a fire going with dry grass, flashing sparks with two rocks, but it didn't work out.

It was a cloudless night and the moon was full, the same moon that the Americans had hopped on two days before. The sky with all its stars had never been closer to me. Everything around me, grass, crickets, the wind, kept me together with all my thoughts, bones and that emptiness in my stomach. I realized suddenly that everything belonged to me, like the hands and legs that I carried with me all the time and that I had learned to use. I put my cigarette behind my ear and didn't even feel the need to smoke.

I heard a panting breath behind me, and when I turned my head, I saw a huge dog near me. If I hadn't felt his tongue on my nape, I would have been sure that he was imaginary, a full-blown hallucination, perfect to report to Dr. Nica. It was pointless to run, he would have torn me up, so I tightened my knees against my chest and placed my head between them, my eyes closed. He licked me on my nape and hands, and once in a while he pushed me with his snout. Strange that

I wasn't afraid; if anything, I was taken over by a kind of exaltation. Then he went away from me and opened his snout, and instead of barking he began howling like a wolf.

Behind me I heard the noise of horse hooves, and I raised my head and saw some tarpaulin carriages that came downhill. They swung like boats lost in waves, no one at the rudder. When they came close to me, the horses stopped by themselves, and a couple of heads showed behind the tarpaulin. The dog ran toward them and let me get up. I could only see their phosphorescent heads under their hats and the edges of their mustaches coming out of their thin faces stretching across the bluish sky behind them. One of them cried something out to me in Hungarian, and when he saw that I didn't answer him, asked me in my language:

"What are you doing here?"

"I need a light," I said, and he pointed me toward him with his cigarette in his mouth. He threw me a matchbox, and I lighted my cigarette with shaking hands. I inhaled deeply into my chest and gave back his matchbox, and I saw his face in the moonlight. It was the gypsy leader who had engaged me the year before, and I had no more doubts when he asked me, as if we had separated only yesterday:

"Where's your wife, where's the elephant?"

"His name is Rajah. I don't know where they are. I'm waiting for them to come any day."

"So what are you doing here at night in the field?"

"I don't know."

"Go and look for them as soon as possible."

He dragged several times out of a pipe that seemed to have been quenched for a hundred years, and when a thick white smoke started coming out of it, he handed it to me like that night in the square. I took two deep drags into my chest. It had a different taste from tobacco but the same pleasant dizziness; deceivingly, it enveloped my head and senses. He shouted something in Roma, and the whole group budged in a racket of crackling wheels, given birth in a twig cage. I heard all of these noises distinctly, as if they'd happened right by my ears.

Behind every tarpaulin rose a head that seemed like Nora's. I started crying to her, but I stopped, because the voice that came out of me wasn't my own. I followed them for a while as if I were tied to them, like those newborn colts that followed them submissively behind their carriages. The same dog appeared again, who now seemed ten times bigger, and he began barking like an angry watchdog. If it weren't the same dog, I think I'd have gone after them all night long. Who says that gypsies steal children?

I went back to the vineyard and lay by grandpa, who slept deeply like all peasants. There are people who go to sleep as soon as it gets dark and wake up at 4 or 5 in the morning, or whenever God shakes their shoulders. I had the most colorful dreams, and in my sleep, I heard how the grapes ripened.

They took his vineyard away after a year. Someone had found out that he'd forgotten about it during nationalization. No one worked it anymore, the vineyard became wild, and after a couple of years, grape-less offshoots stretched all over like strangled vines. People said that they found a dead dog in those wild thickets, who was unable to get out of there, as if he were stuck in a thick cobweb.

Searching for Nora

The next day, I returned to Bistrița, and I knew it wouldn't be long till the circus would come back. I was in an unquiet mood, and it could only have come from that.

I never cared much for premonitions or dreams. I had had horrible, even apocalyptic dreams so often, even I could have foreseen the end of the world or a couple of lesser disasters. They terrified me, but I didn't believe in their power, and as soon as I woke up I shook them off and happily forgot them. I never talked about my dreams and didn't believe in them or my premonitions. These were women's matters. I was also convinced that if you didn't want these to come true, it was good not to talk to anyone about them. They die inside you, or wherever they came from.

Whenever you have a premonition, it's like you always have a thought stuck in a low voltage socket. It's like a current that goes through you continuously, slowly but annoyingly, so that you don't know whether it does you good or ill. That's how I felt in those waiting days.

What's more, I suddenly felt the need to go to the barber's, which had never happened before. I wanted to look good, and I told the barber that I wanted him to shear me carefully. You see yourself best at the barber's, because you have nowhere to look at, and you're endlessly waiting for a new person to come out of the fresh haircut. I told him to shave me a little, and he burst out in laughter. He went twice with his razor over the down beneath my sideburns, and the sensation of the few soft bristles left behind tickled my fingertips.

That night I slept like a log, dreamlessly, and when I got up in the morning, I saw the circus's dome put up. People hastily stretched cords between polls in unbelievable quietness, like professionals who knew exactly what they had to do and couldn't waste a single moment.

The circus still functioned well. Maybe it was the only thing that still worked properly in our world.

In front of the window, the same menagerie with its movable cages filled with stolen lives. Instead of Rajah there was a giraffe that swung its head nervously from one side to the other, like an antenna in the wind. I couldn't see Rajah's trunk and his thick ears anywhere. It's hard to hide an elephant.

I dressed slowly and tactfully, and when I tied my shoes, I saw that my hands were trembling. I put on my white shirt, which I only wore during the end-of-the-year celebrations at school and during holidays. I shined my shoes, as if I were going to church. I decided not to hurry, not to run like crazy to the circus like a desperate person who'd never seen people and animals.

There was great agitation in the square. It was hard to move among those busy people who obviously wanted to start their shows as soon as possible. I didn't see Nora's wagon on wheels, but everything was arranged awkwardly, differently from the year before. I went to the menagerie, and I asked the first person from the circus that I met where the elephant was. They all shrugged, as if the elephant was the last thing on their minds.

The people at the circus are hard to recognize when they're not in their show-costumes, powdered, masked and with wide smiles, as if they were different people. Especially the clowns. The year before, I'd become friends with one who I admired unreservedly, an older fellow who said he wanted to retire. You'd never believe that even clowns want to retire. He had the kind of humor that I liked; he made you laugh in yourself at first, gather all the fun inside until there was no more space for it left and you had to let it all out. Nora said that he was a very lonely person, without family and kids, and that before the war he'd been a pantomime teacher in Paris. A pretty strange art, where people pretend to do things, moving so convincingly that they convince you that they're really doing them. Now that

I think about it, one of them should have become a work-hero in our world a long time ago, but he was a poor clown that some of us barely deigned to laugh at.

I saw him standing on the wagon's steps with a beer bottle in his hand. He had aged a lot, and a clown close to retirement who stares blasé into the void while drinking a bottle of warm beer doesn't offer you a cheerful picture. I got close to him, but he didn't recognize me. He made friends wherever he went, of course; how would he remember me specifically when not even my close aunts recognized me anymore? I'd gotten used to this since I'd grown so much.

"I'm Nora's friend, the trapeze artist girl. Do you know where her wagon is?"

Then he recognized me and slowly and stuffily gurgled in his throat with his whole beer bottle. He looked at me blankly and simply told me, after wiping himself with the back of his hand:

"They're not with us anymore, boy!"

We stared at each other for a long time. He didn't know whether to tell me anything else, and I was unsure whether it would be good to ask him more questions. He stretched his hand into the wagon and took out another bottle of beer, which he opened by slamming the back of his hand on the top against the edge of a stair. Not that I ever saw a beer bottle opened otherwise. He threw his head back and drank it to the bottom, slowly, with his eyes closed, and when he opened them, he didn't like that I was still there.

"They're with the big circus in Moscow." I was quiet. I stared at him, and it was clear that my bubbling eyes gave him some trouble.

"And Nora?"

"The girl stayed in the country."

He stopped talking, as if these things didn't concern me. They were their secrets, part of the itinerant circus. What did I understand, a simple boy from a forgotten town in Transylvania, who waited all year long for the circus to come so that he could have some fun? But I had such an expression that he probably pitied me.

"Look, boy, I see that you're in pain, but the poor girl has had it with the circus. She doesn't even want to hear about it anymore."

I was at a loss for words, and I stood quiet awkwardly, like a poorly cast statue that can't cool. At first, I thought that Nora had died, but the clown had said "poor girl" and you only say "poor" when you talk about living people.

"All right, I'll tell you where she is. I remember the figure from last year with the elephant. I really liked the figure with the elephant. Ha, ha, these things should be done more often, not to mention that there's a circus everywhere these days. Only us clowns still take our job seriously. I can't wait to retire, to hell with it. Well, this girl is unlucky first and foremost because she has such parents. Brainless fools, who wanted to get to the big circus in Moscow no matter what. Not Paris, Rome or London… things have changed, boy. All sorts of crazy people tried the trapeze, just so that someone would notice them."

He handed me the beer bottle, but I didn't like beer. I asked him for a cigarette, which he lighted, and after he took two drags, he handed it to me.

"She said that if you ask about her to tell you she'd like to see you. She said you have things to finish together. She's at Timişul de Sus, the first stop after Brasov. Here's her address."

I smoked as I'd never smoked before, inhaling deep into my chest, everything mixed in a tumult. My head was empty, it didn't exist.

"And the elephant?"

"In any case, he wanted to get out. After the girl left, he disappeared one night, breaking the chain around his leg. He went out into the field somewhere and lay by the grating on a railway. The freight train whistled and whistled in vain; he didn't budge. Not to mention that this was a fast train—it dashed it into pieces, big as it was. The signalman is still looking for him. Anyway, he'd had enough. He was old and cried all the time. Do you want another cigarette?"

I left the poor clown alone and went to the back of the backyard, where I puked for a while. I hadn't eaten, so the only thing that came out of me was poison and the ballast of waiting an entire year. I felt that I'd go upside-down, like clothes that you take off. I didn't know what to do. I was helpless for the first time, and helplessness gives you a special dizziness and disgust that is hard to fight against.

Ionică had forgotten his scythe next to a plum tree, so I took hold of it and started scything the tall grass with a fury that did me good. I cut the hay, grinding my teeth; the yard and the smell of the grass invigorated me. As I cut the grass in which I should have tumbled with Nora, I began to understand that you can't always go against the things that don't go your way, and you have to take them as they come. That grass couldn't hide from the scythe either. It wasn't a revelation, just a simple realization, as when I didn't get up on time in the morning and was late to school. I knew I'd be punished, that I couldn't change anything, but I still ran, panting, thinking that I could turn things around that way.

I had no choice but to go see her. I had some money, there were plenty of trains and stations, I wasn't a wimp anymore and desperation is good for something too, it pushes you forward like a sharp elbow lodged in your ribs. I was furious, and when I went into my house, my sister asked me whether I'd been in a fight with someone. I went up to the attic and took some money I'd managed to save from behind the beam where I'd hidden the sword. I'd wanted to buy a pair of old skis from a neighbor. I went down into the house and put some things into my satchel. I hastily made myself a sandwich with lard, and then I took advantage of the fact that my parents weren't home to leave at once, no monkey business, explanations or threats. But I told my sister, who looked at me frightened, maybe asking herself whether my insanity hadn't come back:

"Tell them I've gone to Timiş for a couple of days. Nora, the daughter of the circus performers, is there. She's my betrothed, you know… I'm not running away from home, tell them this."

I went to Gil's, who lent me some money without questions asked or conditions. I put them all in a hidden pocket in my pants.

I got to the train station too late and too early. My train had just left and the other one was very late. They had a huge map of the country there, and it didn't take long for me to find Brasov and Timişul de Sus. Great luck that we didn't have a big country! I went out into the street, at the edge of the city, where hitchhikers signaled to cars. I started signaling to the cars, and I had a 25 lei bill in my hand. How else would anyone take a kid like me?

A truck that was going to Targu Mures stopped. There was a guy in a not-so-white undershirt at the wheel, who always held an unfiltered cigarette in his mouth which he exchanged with another whenever the ash reached his mouth. I told him I was going to Timis to see a relative. What relative? I didn't tell him, and the guy in the shirt felt that something was off with my story. He wondered at the fact that I'd begun smoking so early, educated boy that I was. Only gypsies' kids drag so heavily from cigarettes, and he told me that doctors had begun saying that all the men in the country would die from smoking. We both seemed like suicide cases that cared for nothing.

I had just begun feeling well in my own skin. It was my first journey into the world and I was in an extreme state of excitement. It's good to travel. The scenery is always changing, and your thoughts change with it. The more you distance yourself from the place where you sleep, wake up, eat, study and drag your tiny life along, the freer and looser you feel, and the carelessness about the world we all step into unknown seemed like a blessing to me. I could be whoever I wanted to be, no one stopped me.

At Targu Mureș, I bought a large ice cream and I ate it on the terrace of a café, where I looked at the people that crossed the street, pressed by their own worries, and I felt good there, above them. I had completely forgotten about Bistrița, about my folks, about school; I was only thinking about Nora, whom I'd see soon. I bought her a large box of chocolates.

Another truck took me to Sighișoara. Another driver in an undershirt who smoked all the time. I told him I was almost 17 and was going to my fiancé in Brașov, a pedagogy student. He said almost nothing. Just before I was about to leave his car, he told me to be careful and not to leave her pregnant. From Sighișoara I caught the express train to Bucharest, which I boarded with a ticket. It was almost empty, and I fooled the ticket collector till Brașov, where I had only two or three stations left.

When we reached the mountains and we passed Timișul de Jos at high speed, I understood that the express train wouldn't stop in Timișul de Sus either. I ran to the rear of the train, and in the last wagon I decisively pulled the alarm signal. The train stopped in a long creaking of the brakes, and when it slowed down enough, I jumped off the train. I rolled several times, but nothing happened to me and I ran through the fir forest. The ticket collector saw me through the window and swore at me loudly, threatening me with the militia, tribunal and prison. I only stopped at the road, which I walked on as if nothing had happened. After a couple of minutes, a militia car came out of nowhere. They asked me if by any chance I had seen a man who ran from the railroad.

It was evening, the sun had set behind the mountains and when I entered Timișul de Sus there was still daylight. I stepped on decisively, like someone who'd arrived there with business on their mind. There weren't too many houses, so I found the one I was looking for easily. It was placed behind a large gate made of cast iron, over which was written in orderly letters: "Recuperation sanatorium" and it was made up of a group of old buildings, joined by alleys with firs and layers of fresh flowers.

You didn't feel that you were near a hospital. All of those buildings had once been luxurious villas, which before the war belonged to rich people who went there from Bucharest. Even the sick people going around in wheelchairs or resting against canes didn't seem completely sick, because they wore street clothes and everything around those villas, mountains, the blue sky and the firs, was so beautiful that suffering and disease were the last thing on your mind. Even this word—sanatorium—no longer inspired something morbid in me, at most some usual lung ailments. It seemed like a place where people went on vacation to forget what they suffer from, a disease that they'd never get rid of and which they wouldn't die from. Death and suffering had no place in such a beautiful place. I sat down on a bench and waited to see her pass by.

I knew it was her mostly from that hairpin, that piece of metal that seemed to have grown right there, on her forehead, and which I think she had never parted with. She had a fuller face, longer, more clear, large shoulders, just as straight, and through her shirt her womanly breasts showed. Most changed of all were her eyes and the glance that came out of them. She no longer had anything of the face of a perpetually tormented child. It was as if joy had nested at the edge of her lips, and I think this is why I didn't notice that she was sitting in a wheelchair that she maneuvered with skill that only someone who'd grown up in the circus could have.

She walked in some circles using the wheels in the back, then she sped toward me, and if I hadn't got up on my feet, she wouldn't have noticed me. She passed by, then she suddenly braked the wheels with her strong hands and turned slowly, unsure whether the ghost she'd passed was really me. We stared at each other for a long time, to make sure we were ourselves and that behind the new faces the same thoughts were hidden.

"If I could get up, I'd come to you."

We were quiet again, searching in vain for words that had run away in fear.

I got close to her and handed her the chocolate box, as if that gesture was very important in that moment and the only reason why I'd gone there. I was acting like a poor messenger who, having reached the end of his journey, doesn't know what else to do.

She only seemed surprised to see me, otherwise she was on top of her game, ready to do something so we'd leave that state of unease. She got close to me and after some time, she took my hand. Just as I often didn't know what people wanted from me at first, I didn't understand what she wanted to do while she pulled me by the hand, trying to make me raise her up or at least help her get to where I was standing stoutly on my feet.

"Today is the first day that I've been able to get up from this chair. I'm sure it's a sign."

"Why are you in it?"

"Because I have no choice for now. Didn't the clown tell you anything? How good! He's an honest man."

She paused and looked at her watch. Then she said, as if we'd just separated yesterday:

"Let's go to the table before the cafeteria closes. I'll tell you everything later."

I wanted to push the chair, but she didn't let me.

"This is a sanatorium for people like me. Of course, not everyone fell from a trapeze. Anyhow, I think I got lucky. I escaped the circus, and starting this fall I'll go to school, but till then…"

"What do you mean you fell?"

"The way you fall in the circus. I was flying between my colleagues. Your hands don't join together in the air and you go down."

"And the net?"

"It was old. Leave these things alone. Now, we have to eat. You're hungry after such a long trip. God, how much you've grown! I almost didn't recognize you."

I went with her to the sanatorium's cafeteria, she sat me at a table and went to speak to a fat man who was a boss there. Inside there were only people in wheelchairs, who sat directly at tables without chairs. It seemed like a world specifically designed for people in wheelchairs. They all seemed to know Nora. She moved among the tables with great dexterity, naturally and confidently, clear-headed and so happy, as if she'd just won an award at the Paralympics. When she came back, she asked me:

"Do you think we two are alike?" I shrugged my shoulders. "I told my boss you're my brother. He says we look alike, ha, ha, ha! He'll bring us a big meal and we'll share it."

A woman wearing an apron stained with every-thing she'd cooked that week brought us a huge plate with fries, chicken and lots of pickles. She caressed Nora on the head protectively, and she cast me a cold and suspicious glance.

"These people are a little scared of my family, after finding out what happened to me."

We ate quietly and gazed at one another. Me glancing at her furtively, like a pickpocket, she looking straight at me, without trying at all to hide that wide and shiny smile that took over her face like a tide starting in her eyes.

"What was I supposed to tell them? That you're my man? No one would have believed me."

"I waited for you all year. Why didn't you write me?"

She didn't answer me. Only the pickles were left on the table, and I finished them loudly, chewing on them meticulously with my teeth, as if they were to blame for everything.

"Let's take a walk," she said. "I want to show you the mountains and the moon. It's a full moon."

We went out to the sanatorium's alleyway and headed toward the cliffs that were a stone's throw away, abrupt like interminable stairs spiraling toward the sky, dimly illumined by blind bulbs and a full and round moon above. I would have liked to hold her hand, but her hands were occupied. We went down winding alleyways until we reached the back of a metallic parapet that completely blocked the passage, as if we'd reached the end of the road. Beyond it there seemed to be nothing but the black emptiness of a chasm, and farther off, other mountains and the starry sky. There were some benches around and the murmur of a brook of mineral water whose name, many years later, I would come across on a label that got very far, like those bottles with messages that desperate people throw into the ocean.

"Help me a little." She got close to a bench and gave me her hands. She pulled me lightly toward herself, and she was finally up close to me. Her legs were shaking like those of baby animals whose first instinct after birth is to run like crazy. She lay on the bench, and I sat by her. We were suddenly equals, like all couples who sit on a bench in the park. She opened the box of chocolates.

"How's Rajah doing?"

So she didn't know anything. The clown really knew how to keep his mouth shut, like a true pantomime artist.

"It's all right. He ran from the circus and they didn't find him anywhere. That's what he wanted, isn't that right?"

Nora nodded her head and didn't say anything, like a wise old man who understands enough. I was glad that she didn't ask me anything else about the elephant, on whose back we'd fallen in love, married and felt for the first time the beguiling gift of freedom. He had been the only witness of our weird pairing. He became dust when he met a freight train. I asked myself whether we weren't somehow untied, now that he'd disappeared.

"Do you think that if he no longer is, we're still as bound together?" This was her question.

"Don't forget the gypsies," I answered her. "They bound us together." Then I told her about the meeting I had several nights before near my grandpa's vine.

"You know how I dreamed about a dog these past nights? He was big and good. He licked my nape and spine, right where I had been broken and I felt it, you understand? I really felt it. I was asleep, and in my sleep I felt his hard tongue everywhere. For several months I felt nothing below my waist, as if that part of the body no longer belonged to me. For several days now it's been different; I've even started moving my legs. Look."

She started to swing her legs lightly to convince me. She struggled to do it, it was obvious, but she seemed happy about the few centimeters that her feet were moving backward and forward, like dead pendulums come to life. Anyway, she seemed slightly disappointed that I couldn't appreciate this miracle as it deserved.

"The doctors can't believe it. They say it's not logical. What do I care for their logic!"

"I don't believe in doctors either. A neighbor made me well."

"What happened to you? Did you fall too, by any chance?"

"No, I didn't fall, but I did have a fall. Now I know it wasn't a big deal."

We were the only ones on the mountainside and it seemed to me that I could hear that huge diapason in my ear again. It was like the diapason of a conductor who wanted to bring me into unison with an unseen choir, with the cliffs and mountain around, maybe with Nora. It was the same one that had often made me going into a torturous resonance, that forced me to stop whatever I was doing to ask foolishly who I was and what the hell I was doing in this world. I hadn't heard it for a long time, and there where we were then, it didn't seem so painful and imperious.

"What are you thinking about? You suddenly have a line on your forehead that I don't recognize."

One could clearly see that I was thinking intensely about something, and too much thinking seemed to me a shameful and ugly abuse back then. Like masturbation. I wanted to tell her about my torturous growing up, about Dr. Nica and the calcium injections, but I changed my mind in time. Once I start telling a story, I can't stop, I have to take it to the end, like a flood that I don't think she needed. The way she lay there serenely, dangling her legs at the edge of the bench, she seemed the happiest being under that full moon.

"Do you hear something?" she asked me. We both stayed quiet, staring at the sky and mountains as if anyone could have come from there.

"My ears are ringing. It's like a huge diapason."

She was the one who said this, and it was clear to me that she was either reading my thoughts or I was transmitting mine to her without wanting to.

"Where will you sleep tonight?" I hadn't thought at all about this, as if beyond that night there was nothing. "I live in a salon with two beds," Nora went on, "and until Monday no one's there. My boss told me that my close relatives can use it. Until recently my grandma stayed with me. You came in time. Next week I'm going to Moscow to another sanatorium. They want to study and treat me there. The doctors say I'm an unusual case."

We were both unusual cases, each with his weirdness, me with my brain, her with her spine, the same spine that we boys, in our idiocy, feared would spill out from our jerking off. I was discovering that in a way, it's good to be an unusual case. Perhaps Nora would get well and walk, and she'd gotten away from the circus. And I was getting better myself, plus I had the advantage of my unseen thoughts.

It's easiest if you can hide your thoughts. It's hard until you learn this trick, then it's simpler than the coin that disappears in the magician's hand. But I hadn't escaped from my circus, but I had no way of knowing that then.

We made our way back to the sanatorium, after I took her in my arms and helped her sit back down in her chair. For a moment she was glued to me; she hugged me quickly and kissed my neck. Her smell—the only thing that hadn't changed at all—awakened my scattered senses, which keep away every trace of a thought from your mind, once they gather together.

It was completely quiet in the sanatorium, as if it had just been evacuated. When I passed through the hallway, she put a finger on her lips, asking me to be quiet. In her tiny salon there were two iron beds, like in hospitals, and pinned on a wall, a postcard from Bistrița in faded, washed-out colors. Some schoolbooks and one of Greek mythology seemed well leafed-through after how thick and messily thrown they were on the table. You can tell a lot about a book that someone's just been through. It's like a ravaged person, having gotten up from bed without having had a chance to comb. Beside this, only the wind with the smell of evergreen wafting around us through the open window and we two, two unusual cases in the course of recovery in a mountain sanatorium.

"You can sleep on the left bed. We also have a bath and sink. Wash there."

Love Story

I took off my clothes in the narrow bathroom, and I washed myself the way she told me to, at the sink. I had some fresh acne on my face that I tried not to touch. I put on my shirt with Che Guevera's hairy head and sat on the bed. Nora wasn't inside anymore. She reappeared after half an hour with her hair wet, in a white nightgown. For the first time, I saw her without that obstructive hairpin, and her black hair flowed beautifully over her forehead and shoulders. She helped herself with her hands and, in a leap, she was in the bed.

"You turn off the light." I flipped the switch of a pale bulb that didn't change what we could and couldn't see much. The full moon outside was more powerful. She handed me the box of chocolates, and for a while only the rustling of the wrapping paper and our nervous chewing could be heard.

"How about you come next to me?"

I didn't wait for long and stretched alongside her. Hospital beds are narrow and deep, like strange hammocks suspended on all sides in an outside world like spiderwebs. You sink into them and you're afraid that you can't get out. They squeak and move along with you in all directions. If it could talk, you wouldn't want to listen to a hospital bed's story, with all the horrible things that went on in there.

Ours creaked with every movement like a poorly tuned instrument that tries to say something. It was obvious that it had never held two people like us before. I was glued to her because I couldn't be otherwise. She'd perfumed herself. Where could she have found perfume in the sanatorium? She took me by the hand and pulled the blanket from off her feet, revealing herself. Then she started to move her fingers, soles, then her thighs and slowly her hips, which seemed a little emaciated.

"Last week I couldn't do this. It's incredible, don't you think? I'm much better from the waist up."

I was quiet, looking at her body, which she was revealing slowly, taking her nightgown off. She was completely naked, and a knot formed in my throat. She was beautiful. The ditches between her ribs had filled up, and her breasts were like those of Greek statues—I'd even dare say she beat Aphrodite when it came to breasts and curves in general. That goddess born in sea foam—if you looked at the pictures in books—was kind of too fat for my taste.

"Imagine that I'm one of those sirens that tempted Odysseus, because I exist more from the midpoint up. For the time being. I read that he asked his friends to tie him to a mast so he wouldn't let himself fall into temptation."

There was nothing to tie yourself to in a sanatorium's room, but it was good exercise for the imagination.

"Who's that hairy guy on your chest?"

"Jimmy Hendrix."

"Whoever that is, take it off. He doesn't belong with us in the bed."

I took off my shirt and took her by the hand. She put my hand on her hard breasts, which were exactly the size of my hand. I felt them so well, as if they'd grown in my palms. Her odor invaded my body like a dizzying heat. We kissed as we'd never kissed before, and I was good when it came to this. At last, everything I had learned that year proved useful, and after the way in which she closed her eyes and breathed fast and deep, I understood that she really appreciated my skill.

I had on some large underwear that rose like a small tent, and she went into them with her hand, slowly, like a hungry snake in search of eggs. She caressed me everywhere, squeezing me hard without hurting me. She didn't know what to do and did everything that went through her head, because I had been her man for over a year. Suddenly, I sighed inhumanly. Then she turned and succeeded in pulling one of her hips over me. She pulled me lightly over her even though I was resisting her somewhat, not because I didn't want it but because I was afraid to crush her, to break something in that hurt siren's body of hers.

"Come over me."

I felt how she was struggling to open her legs, whose muscles were learning how to rise again. I helped her.

"Come, come into me. Don't be scared."

I listened to her. I entered her slowly, carefully, as one must enter into a woman he cares for. Everything I did that night was like coming to the end of a long waiting period that finally came to fruition, not as we had hoped, but that came to fruition. She was happy that she could move her legs somewhat, and I was happy because I had somehow reached a denouement that had pressed me heavily, on which my entire future manhood seemed to depend.

We did it many times that night. We would wait only so long as to catch our breath, our eyes nailed to the ceiling, or to swallow a piece of chocolate or two, and then we'd start over. Each time it lasted longer, and we got further. She couldn't get enough of the fact that she could feel and strain somewhat under my body. After I convinced myself that I wasn't breaking anything in her, I couldn't stop going there where I had dreamt so much to go, that endless tunnel of juicy fog, of life and death. It was clear to me that the pairing of two bodies is linked to both, because we felt as if we were going into another world, passing suddenly with our senses through a forbidden wall.

Every time I finished, I got dizzy and sighed deeply. She would ask each time: "How was it, my love?" as if we had just returned from another fantastic journey. We both sighed like wounded animals who lick and heal their wounds. We stopped toward the morning because she was bleeding lightly, but she told me not to worry because nothing hurts her, and this is what happens with virgins. It's like something too full spills over from too much waiting.

I took her to the toilet, where I had to hold her hand while she urinated happily in front of me for a long time. Everything made her happy—that she was bleeding like a grown up girl, that it didn't hurt, that she could urinate whenever she wanted, like before, but especially that I was the witness of all these rare events of life, which were given to us, so we can learn how to be happy out of nothing.

She spoke like a clever girl from the South. Faster and outspoken, unlike us, the northern Transylvanians, she knew how to press on some words that suddenly became heavier and came out differently than all the nothingness that people usually tell each other. We both wanted to give more than we got; otherwise you couldn't reach that condition. How many years would pass before I'd get there again! This gift grows on the secret shore of those who no longer fear drowning. Only two children like us could get out safe even recovered, from that sanatorium of those wounded without a cure, a place that no one could escape.

On the second day, I got up staring at the sun. Nora had left for the treatment, where those doctors who didn't believe in her healing, because it wasn't possible in any of the books they'd read, waited for her. I heard that some doctors even get angry when their patients heal despite their prognoses, or when they stubbornly continue to live when they have only a little while left.

I remained a sick man without a diagnosis or prognosis, which is what all people are after all. I walked along in the sanatorium's alleys, and it seemed sad to me to see so many cripples. What saddened me most wasn't their illnesses, crutches or wheelchairs as much as their drained faces, into which suffering had dug deep and dry gutters where not even tears flowed anymore. Nora didn't belong to this world. I reached the parapet where we had been the night before and drank lots of mineral water from "the spring of wonders." That's what it was called, and the old inscription, almost faded, had been put there in different times, when people still believed in miracles and helped to bring them about.

At the spring, I was alone with an abandoned wheelchair. Who would abandon a wheelchair? There was no one around, and I thought that maybe a miracle had occurred, and whoever was using it got up and simply left. It's just that I'm afraid to believe in miracles.

I sat on the chair and tried to move with it, trying to imagine what it was like to be crippled. I got scared, thinking that there could be reverse miracles too, where something miraculously bad happens. I got up and ran, happy that I had legs that listened to me.

Nora was outside in the sun waiting for me. She had so much life in her eyes that she didn't resemble the person I'd met a year before at all. I wanted to kiss her, but I remembered that I was her brother.

"I want us to go take a walk on the road," she said. I pushed the wheelchair down the mountain road, which snaked its way toward Predeal. A warm wind, with the odor of firs, waved her free-flowing hair. That hairpin had disappeared as if it had never been. She held one of her hands over my hands as a sign that she was there, close to me, and everything that happened the night before was real in every detail. I was very serious, frowning even; she flashed a smile. Once in a while a car would pass by and we'd see the faces of drivers who stared at us in bewilderment, as if they'd never seen two people like us there before. Where the serpentine climb began there was a restaurant named Cotul Donului with tables outside, and I pushed her to one of them.

"I have money," I told her, "and I want us to eat here." We were the only clients, but no waiter came for a good while. In the end, a pretty bitter woman came, who told us she didn't have much in the kitchen. I ordered some draft beer and cabbage rolls with an expert flourish. I lit a cigarette that I'd prepared since the day before and I smoked quietly, now and then wiping the foam of the beer, which wasn't bad at all.

"Whatever the case might be, in the fall, I'm coming back from Moscow and I want to take school seriously. I want to become a doctor."

I looked at her surprised, as if she'd just made a gaffe. She was obsessed with the future, this was it, meaning she thought seriously about what was to come, things that I couldn't see at all, as if I were blind on the inside. The future didn't exist for me, even though high school admissions were about to come. I couldn't look over the fence of the present day, the only dimension I could touch.

"I'll stay with my grandma in Constanța. Have you ever been to the Black Sea?"

"No. This is the farthest I've ever travelled."

"Everyone gets to the sea sooner or later. When you go, you'll find me there."

We ate, looking at each other in silence. The waitress sat with her elbows on the windowsill, smoking and eyeing us with that look belonging to simple people who have no idea what to think about what they see. It was obvious that she was curious. She came and took our empty plates. She seemed more welcoming; she was nice even, though kind of old. She was around 35.

"Don't ask for any more beer. I do have some good and juicy savarins." I asked her for two, and I wondered at the fact that she didn't ask us whether we had enough money. When she brought it to us, she looked at us for a long time, smiling, and she said:

"Who are you, kids? There's something about you, I don't know what… as if you just escaped from somewhere. No one really runs away these days. We're all hammered nails. Anyway, you're cute. But what's the matter with you?"

"Nothing's wrong with us, ma'am." I wanted to go on a long tirade, but I refrained.

The waitress looked at us strangely, neither nicely nor nastily. She didn't know what to believe, because it was clear that we hadn't run away from home and that we weren't liars. Who would have run away from home in a wheelchair? Maybe we really were true escapees, but we didn't realize it. Nothing seemed to match what she'd started thinking about us. I wanted to pay, but she didn't want to take any money.

We left slightly puzzled, understanding that the world was looking at us with curious eyes. On the road, the sun came out again, and we went along a path that led to the river. Nora wanted to be by the water. I took her in my arms and stretched her on the riverbank, supporting her on a boulder. I lay by her, and we both sat back and looked at the sky. A river that murmurs next to you has a hypnotic effect, so we both went into a kind of trance. We held hands, and I'm sure that we were both doing the same thing: flying over mountains at a low altitude. Then we'd turn again on our backs, and over us the cupola of the sky was like the huge cupola of a circus.

We stayed there till evening came, without making a sound. Words had run away with the sun's rays, but we didn't really need words anymore. Before leaving, we kissed, but it was a pretty sad kiss, though it excited us greatly despite the tears that were drowning us. If so many trucks hadn't passed by on the road, I'd have taken off her clothes, and we would have made love right there, on the river's boulders.

I was sad, but my mood was more one of rebellion because I didn't know against whom to rebel; I felt like howling like a half-tamed wolf. I got up and started to throw wide stones nervously over the surface of the water, making bets in my head on the number of circles the stone would make before sinking. If it makes more than three jumps, I'll see Nora again in my life. One, two, three, splash. One, two, three, splash. It wasn't bad. I calmed down a little.

"Let's go, my love."

It sounded so good! No one had spoken that way to me before. The girls from the South knew how to talk, and if they loved you they weren't embarrassed to tell you. I took her in my arms as if I'd done that my entire life and placed her carefully on the wheelchair.

We went back to the sanatorium, sat at the same table in the cafeteria, and the cook brought us chicken, fries and pickles again. It was pretty noisy around, though there weren't many people.

"Have you heard about Mrs. Stan?" the cook asked Nora.

"Heard what?"

"They found her wheelchair by the spring. She jumped over the parapet. She left you a note in your room."

I had to go with Nora to her room, where there was a bag and a handwritten note on her bed. In the bag there was a French perfume, the same as the one she had used the night before, and a pair of snake-skin high-heels.

"She was my best friend. She didn't have much left to live and she didn't want to live. I liked her perfume, and I told her that one day I'll walk in high-heeled shoes."

Nora didn't cry, but her eyes were full of tears. She opened the perfume bottle and smelled it, breathing deep into her chest, as if Mrs. Stan's spirit dwelled inside her. Then she asked me to put the high-heels on her feet. One could tell they were old and well-made, as things were made in other times. Shoes like these could be heirlooms. They were made in Paris; it was written on them. I put them on her feet carefully, as on a Cinderella with problems, and I helped her get up. They fit her. She tried to make two steps, and with my help she somehow made it. Then another two. If she had been on the moon, like that American astronaut, it would have been much easier for her.

That night we had a different spirit within us. Calmer, better, less extreme. We never spoke again about our elephant, and Nora didn't utter another word about Mrs. Stan. They too were perhaps some kind of refugees.

I smoked in the room with the open window, and then I lay by her on the bed, quiet, calm, but as drained as after a hard competition. One that I had feared much, precisely because I was the only competitor. The truth is that for the first time I felt like a conqueror. It was good, though it wasn't at all clear to me what the stakes were in the end. I was convinced that I passed through a kind of wall.

"Do your folks know where you are?" Nora asked me.

"No." I hadn't thought about them at all. Mom was crying for sure, breaking her hands in the kitchen, and dad was chain-smoking nervously. After all, I had run away from home, that's what I'd done.

"I think it's good for you to go back tomorrow. In two days, I'll leave too."

A great peace surrounded us both, which blended with the mountains and the high sky outside. We were afraid to spoil it by resorting to words. We finished the last chocolate bars, supported by the iron grating of the bed. Nora took the perfume bottle and applied some to her neck and behind her ears. She did it with an absent flourish, as if she'd done this every evening for years. In the meantime, she stared at nothing. A nothingness I felt in my stomach like a denser continuation of the peace we'd gone into.

"Kiss me."

We kissed differently than before; we almost bit one another, because our lips were tighter, and the tremor that came out of us with each breath was a mist that excited us past telling. I went into her with my eyes closed, clenching my teeth, sighing. She scratched my back deeply with her nails, but it didn't hurt. When we finished, we both cried. We fell asleep as we were, naked, and when we got up, Nora had the salt of dried tears on her face, the traces of those tiny snails of sadness.

That's how the head nurse found out when she barged into the room at around 7 AM. Her pages fell from her hand, and she almost let out a cry of amazement and indignation. I pulled the sheet over us and waited to see what would happen.

"I thought you said he's your brother. Aren't you ashamed?"

"I'm sorry I lied to you, ma'am. He's my man."

"What man? You're just two sniveling fools playing with fire. This is why you're saying you're getting better, only that 'therapies' like these aren't allowed in sanatoriums. Have you thought about what you'd do if you got pregnant?"

That's when I felt the need to talk, to defend Nora, to yell a bit at that woman who'd barged into our lives. To tell her the truth. It's much easier for me to speak to strangers, to people I'm seeing for the first time and that I know I won't see again. They seem like creatures made specifically for you to throw the truth in front of them.

"Ma'am, she's my wife, and I can't allow you to speak to her this way."

"Wife...?" she started laughing nervously, until her glasses fell off her nose, and she looked more and more curiously at me.

"We married last year."

"Can you show me the certificate?"

"We won't show you anything, ma'am. And please leave the room so we can get dressed."

She didn't leave, but neither did she say anything, and she continued to stare at us, oscillating between anger and amusement. Then I got out of bed, butt naked as I was, with a morning hard-on that was just starting to die down, and I put on my clothes in front of her as if she wasn't there. Slamming the door, she left us alone because in the end she didn't know how to react.

We didn't know what to do from then on either. Something had ended. This was clear to us. As if we'd read everything in a book and we were scared to go on and flip the pages.

Through the wide-open window, the same ringing diapason that it seemed we could both hear came from the mountains. It no longer scared me; now it seemed more like the whistling of an umpire who tries to re-establish an order that never existed.

I wanted to help her get dressed, but she didn't let me. For the first time, Nora had something tired and extenuated on her face, like a marathon runner who could barely stand on her feet after crossing the finish line. We were both two exhausted champions, that's what we were. She pulled some elastic socks slowly over her calves, which went up to under her knees and which till evening, when I'd be gone, would leave deep marks on her skin, like the traces of a strangulation. I wanted to pull those firm socks lower, but she sopped my hand. I felt the need to protect her, to spoil her, but she didn't really want to let herself be spoiled anymore.

She'd retreated into herself. She dressed in silence without looking at me, as if I weren't there.

"You have to go back home," she said, staring at the floor.

"I know."

We went to the train station and got a ticket for a train that would come get me in two hours. I had no idea how could we spend those last minutes that we had left. Beyond them, nothing was in our control. When it's skimped and counted in this way, time passes through your body like an electric current that has nowhere to flow. You hear it ticking from one ear to the other.

"You have to eat something," she said to me.

"Yes, I have to eat."

I pushed the wheelchair almost at a running pace to the restaurant we'd been to the day before, and we sat at the same table. No one was there. At one point, the waitress showed up; she looked like she'd just gotten up, barely out of bed. With her blouse poorly buttoned over her large breasts, she seemed to be in a good mood.

"I saw you through the window, kiddos. What's up with you so early?"

"His train leaves in an hour and he has to eat something. He has a long way back home." Nora spoke like a worried wife whose husband is about to go to war.

"I'll make you two omelets—on the house."

A man in an undershirt also lived over the restaurant; half-leaning on his windowsill, he was smoking quietly, gazing at us indifferently. The waitress returned fast with two omelets and some coffee.

"And why do you have to leave?" she asked me.

"Because that's what has to happen."

I started eating nervously, looking into the plate, continuing to gobble up the omelet, like it was very important for me to eat right then. The woman didn't say anything after that. She didn't want to mix herself up anymore in our story, which seemed complicated and turbid. She didn't want to take my money this time either, and before we left, she kissed us both. She wanted to do something for us, but she didn't know what.

Back on the road, we didn't say anything. We were scared of words, as if they'd all become poisonous. I walked slowly, indifferently, my mind emptied, manfully defying the few minutes I had left till the train's arrival. I went into the train station at the same time as it. I had to notice that the new locomotive, which was electric, like a big box on wheels, was nevertheless a trustful thing that I could hand my new life to and that which was to come.

When it whistled, I went up the steps of the nearest wagon. All the trains leave with a weird jolt, and if you're not careful you can go and stay at the same time. When the train started moving, Nora pushed herself with both her arms and got up on her feet. She waved at me for a long time, without holding on to anything. That's how I'd always remember her.

The locomotive continued to whistle until the station in Timişul de Sus was gone.

I stayed in the corridor of the wagon almost the entire trip, with my head out the window. The wind was doing me good. Besides my hair, it was also blowing the tangled curls of my thoughts, which would regroup whenever the train stopped, scolding me because I had gone like a coward, leaving Nora in a sanatorium where she was learning how to walk again.

I wasn't sure whether it wasn't more so the regret that the night would come and that I would no longer be able to smell her body, to make love to her, feel that growing dizziness that made me almost faint with pleasure. There's surely something divine in lovemaking with a woman, but I had yet to learn that this wasn't true of any woman. I was once again alone, and I felt as abandoned as hell.

I didn't feel like going into my compartment, because inside it were two lovers who were kissing like crazy and they made me feel sick. I couldn't see lovers for a long time. I hadn't even observed until then that there are so many people around who love one another or who at least hold each other's hands and gaze at one another in a special way. I couldn't bear going to the movies either, especially the French-Italian ones. The American movies with cowboys were different; people there shot each other, and even when love reared its head here and there, it was duller and manlier, not all tears and sighs like with us.

Half of Transylvania passed before my eyes and I passed it all through her eyes, lips, hair, odor and crippled legs. Nora had gone into me again, but this time through another door. I would hold her in me for a long, long time.

The End of the Circus

When I reached Bistrița, it was evening. Everything was as I'd left it, or at least so it seemed. The boys were outside on the maidan, plotting something in front of Pişta's house. When they saw me, they left everything they were doing and surrounded me with looks that reminded me of their admiration from the year before when I ran away with Nora and the elephant.

"Your father is very furious," they warned me. "Everyone knows you ran away from home."

I stayed with them till night came. They were upset at the people from the menagerie because they hadn't paid them the money they promised for some fish they fished at the waterfall, which the circus ordered to feed two poor pelicans that refused to eat any more canned fish. They were planning on bombing with stones the barracks where the people who broke their promise were sleeping.

"The circus isn't how it used to be," they said. "The schedule is bad, the clowns aren't in the mood and one of the lions ate the arm of a maniacal trainer because he whipped him badly."

I was much more afraid of my folks' reaction and the circus I was about to have in my own house.

I went in on tiptoe, as if I could have passed by unnoticed. I didn't know what to expect. The sturdy slap dad gave me as soon as he spotted me convinced me that there was no point in expecting something good. Mom too slapped me on the other cheek, to balance me out. I couldn't believe she could have such a heavy hand. She'd never slapped me like that. But their faces, green from rage and so much waiting, horrified me most. My sister had hidden in a corner and was gazing at me curiously, as at a convicted person.

They took turns giving me a long speech about the garbage life that I was painstakingly preparing for myself, about the debauchery that had gotten deep into my bones, like a plague that I wouldn't be able to escape. They had understood my caprices up till then, which had worried them; but this time it went too far. My mind was shaping like a soft clay. My folks decided to curb the evil at the root, so they'd slap me again, as if those roots would just come out of me. They were sure that if I wouldn't start studying, I'd wind up caring for the pigs in Sigmir, a farm where only gypsies worked. Or maybe a correctional facility, or maybe even prison. I had to think well about what I'd do; life is hard and unforgiving, and without studying, school and discipline, I'd be done for good. In the best case scenario, they'd recruit me in the army and teach me what life means there. I'd come out a "man", brainwashed, with a cigarette butt smoldering at the corner of my lips, plus some wrong drunken tattoos. "Look, this is what we see you're heading for," they kept on repeating. In the end, they yelled as long as they could that the circus and the circus performers' daughter were only in my head. They only existed there, pure delusions of my mind.

I lacked the strength to confront them. I grabbed a blanket and ran outside. I stopped only once I got to the back of the orchard. In a way, I understood their anger, but I didn't give a damn about the foggy future that, of all the people in the world, had chosen me. I was full of Nora; I had no space for anything else. I knew she wasn't a delusion.

I lay down where I'd sat with her the year before, and the mowed lawn smelled just as disturbing. Those grass blades were the descendants of the grass on which I'd sat with her, and that dizzying odor was a continuation of my dream about her. Unclear thoughts were going through my head, troubling images that no longer scared me. I had gotten used to the corners of my own mind. I had come to understand that there was nothing bad in that labyrinth where I would get lost so easily. The only thing was not to go too deep into it.

I went back inside to scrounge a cigarette from dad and found myself with another pair of parental slaps. This time I lost my temper.

"If you touch me one more time, I'll really run away from home." I don't know whose hand exactly slipped, but then I let loose furiously, nearly knocking the door out of its hinges.

"Good bye to you!" That's all I told them, and I left determined, with that determination that leaves a strong whirlwind behind, which makes those whose door you slammed in their noses pause a while and respect you. Later on I did this many times, because it puts you into a good, manly mood.

In the back of the orchard, it was quiet, and nothing could be heard but the murmur of the leaves and my nervous exhalations, which filled the air with cigarette smoke. This is exactly what I'd do; I'd run away from home. With the circus. Nora hated the circus; I liked it. Searching for her, I'd travelled alone for the first time and discovered the joy of wandering, which fit me wonderfully. Suddenly I felt like another person, free, master of myself and my changing fate, which in this way gained a kind of invulnerability. Moving from one place to another, you can fool the future, which loses sight of your tracks and doesn't know where to find you anymore. Maybe I had the soul of a loafer.

I lay on my back on the mown hay, put my hands behind my back and gazed for a long time at the starry sky. The big dipper, the small dipper, the Evening Star, the

Milky Way, the moon conquered by the Americans, so much scary space above me, so much space to run away with your mind. And God, somewhere between all these, surely busy with other things more important than mine.

Tomorrow I will go straight to the circus and offer my services. When you have a clear plan in your head, everything gets simplified. It was hot, and I fell asleep dreaming of Nora, who tightly filled all that unknown space that the universe was yawning above me.

In the morning, my sister brought me something to eat and counseled me not to test their patience too much. I'd done more than that already, dear sister, so I left straight to the circus, where I came across the old clown. I had a healthy rage in me, constructive and controlled, such as I'd never had before. I wondered at my mad courage, because it had something in common with madness, no doubt. I had read somewhere that true madmen don't realize this, and that's when you feel like asking yourself where the border is between madness and normalcy, who determines it and where it passes. And what's this border like?

When I told the clown what I wanted to do, he started drinking warm beer again. Because I spoke like a grown man on business, he seemed to take me seriously. After he obliterated two or three bottles, he told me that they needed people. They were growing through a slight personnel crisis because the circus, he said, had become a way of life for many, and they didn't want to stay under that canvas cupola anymore.

He took me to the manager, a guy in an undershirt who asked me how old I was. I said 18, and he pretended to believe me.

"What can you do?"

"I know how to make people laugh."

The clown suddenly glanced at me with interest.

"I could let him assist me," he said.

"Give him a window to carry," said the manager. The clown put out his cigarette, a real filthy one, and he grabbed an imaginary window, not too large but heavy, and handed it to me. I immediately went into his pantomime: I took the window that was making me bow-legged because of how heavy it was, and I slipped between the poles there until I shattered it in a thousand shards, which I started to pick up carefully. They stopped me so I wouldn't cut myself, from which I deduced that it wasn't bad.

"Come tomorrow so we can discuss."

It sounded like a deal, and I felt doubly manly. Suddenly, the little fury I still had at my folks passed, and I thought to tell them somehow about my new job till the circus would leave. And me with it.

During the day, I loafed in the maidan with the boys, who were insisting I speak. This time they also felt that something had happened. It could be read clearly on my forehead. They gave me cigarettes, and Gil, after I told him that I was leaving with the circus, invited me respectfully to an ice cream. He would almost have, but he was a loner. He didn't need to run away with a circus, he would say;

he wanted to run away from the circus of everyday life. He admired me anyway, just because I wanted to wander the world. I didn't say anything to the others. The whole gang was against the circus, which not only invaded their territory but didn't even let them enter without tickets. They pelleted them with pebbles every night, and the Podaru brothers were the most set against them.

In the evening, they let me go to the show without a ticket, but they seemed weaker than the year before, even though they were doing about the same thing. The old clown tried; it was obvious. When he needed a spectator, he took me out of the first row and used me in one of his tricks. He took some long knives from his waist and explained to the public with his pantomime that they would fly by my head before sticking into a beam. He blindfolded me and asked me to not move. I knew the trick. People ran away from the start, but I stayed unmoved there, and he pretended to get ready to throw the knives. I had to do something funny; after all, I wanted to become a clown. I started to grimace, pretending to be scared, crossing my legs as if I were ready to soil myself from fear. The public started laughing softly, until one of the knives planted itself near my left temple. When I heard the dry sound of the blade lodging itself so close to my thoughts, I almost did soil myself. No one laughed anymore. I assumed a troubled reverence, as if I'd expected this, and I started running with my eyes blindfolded, because I knew where the exit was, and I didn't want to see the clown's face.

I stopped in the back of the orchard, where I thought suddenly that maybe everyone had gone nuts, only they didn't realize it, and no one took them to a psychiatrist or injected them with calcium. I had a moment of doubt at the thought that maybe they had tested me. They wanted to see whether I would take them seriously, whether I was more than a worthless loser who wanted to take on the sea with his finger. They didn't need people like these nowadays, now that everything was a kind of circus, monkey business and mockery.

Maybe there was another circus inside the circus we all saw in the evening under the cupola. One hidden from the glances of the unskilled, the real circus. Perhaps I would become a knife thrower after all. Nora had surely belonged to that real circus. Too bad that she of all people had such bad luck.

"Hey, come and sleep inside!" mom called to me from the veranda, and after the tone of her voice, I felt that things had gotten better. She gave me food without saying anything, and after I finished, she asked me if I wanted more, which she never did. She'd always complained that she'd grown tired of cooking food from nothing and that one day she wouldn't know what to put in the dish.

"You've lost weight like a greyhound."

I went to bed carefully next to dad, who pretended to sleep. We all pretended to sleep for about two hours, then we opened our eyes because, though barely past midnight, too much light was coming through the window.

It took me a while to understand that the circus was on fire. The flames that came out of the thick canvas of the cupola seemed to come from somewhere deep, from an older fire that had kindled a long time ago. I sprinted outside in my pajamas, but I didn't get too far because the whole circus was burning and throwing off sparks and a deadly blaze. The firemen had come; lacking water, they assisted helplessly in consuming my future.

They evacuated the circus performers who couldn't do anything against the fire. They freed the animals from the menagerie. Their hair shaggy, they went each and every way through the maidan, afraid of their unexpected freedom. The two lions died burned in their cages, because no one dared to open the door.

I sat helplessly in front of the house, my hands to my back like an old wise man who finally seems to understand something. My folks stared out the window, and the flames that shone on their faces gave them the aura of frightened saints.

There was nothing else left to do. Someone handed me a cigarette, which I lit with a fuming splinter. I went to smoke it in the rear of the orchard. There, the giraffe was eating quietly from the top of a tree—forgotten plums, which no one had been able to pick.

ADRIAN SANGEORZAN was born in 1954 in Romania. He graduated from the Medical School at the University of Cluj and worked as a doctor in communist Romania until 1990 when he immigrated to the United States. He lives in New York and works as a specialist in Obstetrics and Gynecology.

His volume of memoirs and fiction titled *Between Two Worlds—Tales of a Women's Doctor* was published in two editions and got the Prize for Fiction in Romania. The book came out in the US with the title *Exiled from the Womb—Tales of a Women's Doctor*.

He is the author of several novels and collections of short stories: *Vitali, Among Women, The Tap on the Shoulder*, and collections of poetry: *Over the Lifeline, Voices on a Razor's Edge*, (exquisite corpse poems with Carmen Firan), *The Anatomy of the Moon, The Span of Memory, Masked World*, all bilingual-editions Romanian-English. He is co-translator of *Naming the Nameless/Locul Nimănui—An Anthology of Contemporary American Poetry*. He is a member of the Romanian Writers Guild and the American International Library of Poets. www.adriansangeorzan.com

Translator PAUL BOBOC was born in 1993 in Baia Mare, Romania. He moved with his family to the United States in 2001. He earned a B.A. in English Literature from Boston College, and an M.A. in English Literature from Brandeis University, where he focused on Renaissance literature with emphasis on the dramas of Shakespeare. He translated into English several Romanian writers and a seminal work of Romanian prose, Nicolae Steinhardt's *Jurnalul Fericirii* (*The Journal of Joy*) due to be published in 2022. He teaches History, English Language Arts and Social Studies at Central Jersey College Prep Charter School in Somerset, NJ.

www.ingramcontent.com/pod-product-compliance
Lightning Source LLC
Chambersburg PA
CBHW030817020726
47499CB00006B/1960